RED HOT LOVER
By Mel Teshco

Thank you to all the readers who continued on with book 3 of Winged & Dangerous!

MEL TESHCO

Cover Art by Kellie Dennis at Book Cover by Design
www.bookcoverbydesign.co.uk[1]

---

1. http://www.bookcoverbydesign.co.uk

Chapter One

Zahlee sucked in a breath and held her outstretched wings steady. Hot, blustery wind streamed past. Adrenaline burned through her veins, not quite neutralizing the icy shivers of alarm shooting up and down her spine.

The ground blurred just meters beneath her soaring, outstretched body but she was going too fast for touchdown now. She'd pushed her ability to the limit, trusted in her flight instincts to beat her lover at his own daring.

Oh, god. I'm not going to make it.

Then the rocky, arid Australian ground dotted with parched grasses abruptly dropped away. Her dancing shadow disappeared into the vast emptiness of a deep valley below and she sailed high through the air, the treetops a distant green below.

She let loose a discordant, exhilarated laugh that dispersed into the bright midday air as a whole different adrenaline overtook her.

Steele, her gargoyle lover, closed in from behind.

An updraft snatched them high. As they leveled out Zahlee wheeled to the left, back into the updraft that would take her higher still. Steele followed, his webbed wings, slightly larger than her eight-foot wingspan, deftly manipulating the thermal currents.

She closed her eyes for a moment, dizzy not from the ever-shrinking scenery below but the delicious lust ricocheting through her naked body and making her pulse race.

This was living! No clothes. No cares. Just the open sky. And the man—gargoyle—ready to take her.

The wind blew along the crease of her pussy, tightening her nipples harder still. Her long hair that she'd snagged into a topknot, whipped errant, dark curls in front of her face, blinding her to Steele as his big hands locked on to her shoulders.

Her pulse pounding in her ears, she moaned, so turned on his touch alone almost sent her into orgasm.

His wings snapped in the air just above hers as he spread her legs with one muscled, hard thigh. His cock teased the opening of her pussy for just a moment, where nerve endings tingled and throbbed with anticipation.

This was just what she needed—who she needed? Her breath caught on a half sob. She didn't want anyone else but Steele. Certainly not the human lover she'd abandoned so many years ago.

Saul Daniels.

Her belly clenched. She'd promised herself to never think of him again.

Fool. She'd thought of little else.

Steele pulled her back. She gasped as his cock speared deep into her tight, wet cunt. And already close to the edge, she instantly climaxed, crying out as Steele rocked inside her then came right after her, his hot seed shooting deep into her contracting pussy.

Their midair fuck had to be brief. They were losing altitude fast.

Steele's hands clasped her face from behind. Still joined, he angled her head so that his mouth could settle on hers in a swift, hard kiss that stamped her as his in the most fundamental way.

Then his head reared back. She glimpsed the flash of his possessive gaze and something else shadowed beneath—a dark, hidden emotion that sent her senses into overdrive.

Something was wrong.

Her breath hissed as he abruptly disengaged. His hand moved to claim hers as he skimmed through the air beside her, carefully elevating his wings above hers.

A clearing, aptly named "the strip", which the *Triskellon* clan frequently used to land safely, came into sight.

She sneaked a sideward look at her lover, her belly churning. She was all too aware he wanted the one thing she couldn't give, the only thing.

Her love.

His expression radiated intensity. And though he was a passionate, hot-blooded male, particularly after sex, there was a set hardness to his face this time, a tension along his jawline.

Her heart dropped. It should have been all too easy to love him, indeed, there were plenty of women who did. Only, she couldn't give that part of herself.

It had already been taken.

In unison they folded their wings, their legs dropping vertically underneath. He released her hand as they landed with knees bent and their wingtips meeting before compressing together at the back.

They walked together noiselessly through the towering gums, bunya pines and wattle trees where fierce sunlight barely peeked through the foliage overhead. Unable to take the suffocating silence one second longer, she clasped his forearm and drew him to a stop beside her. "Steele, what's wrong?"

He looked ahead, his nostrils flaring as he echoed, "What's wrong?" He twisted toward her, his waist-length, dark hair swishing across his spine, concealing the word *Triskellon* that had been seared into his skin. His blue-green eyes burned like the sun glinting on the surface of the deep sea. "I'm in love with a woman who is in love with someone else."

Her breath caught. So things were out in the open. At last.

She couldn't deny his words. She was still in love with Saul no matter how much she tried to deny it. That Steele was obsessed with her wasn't any surprise. She'd seen it in his every longing look, his every tender touch and every fierce mating.

Steele *should* have been her perfect mate. Not only was he the most powerful member of the *Triskellon* clan—making him their natural-born leader—he was intelligent, handsome as sin, courageous and loyal.

He could also be controlling, unyielding and more than a little manipulative. In general those were great attributes to possess as gargoyle leader but those very "qualities" had been to Zahlee's detriment. "I...I don't know what to say," she whispered.

"Don't say anything," he rasped. "I know you still want your human."

She shook her head in denial. Steele could never learn the truth. Already his love for her teetered dangerously close to obsession. It would be stupid, reckless, to acknowledge his suspicions. "No! No, I—"

"You screamed *his* name at the height of orgasm," he growled thickly. "You were thinking of him, not me."

Oh, dear god. She closed her eyes, forcing back a hot flush of fear. "Steele...I'm sorry."

"Don't." His eyes glowed, hot and reproachful. His hands moved to her shoulders, his grip fierce. "Don't dare feel sorry for me." Pride was stamped on his face. "That is the one thing I could not forgive you for."

Zahlee stayed mute and still as he nodded once, then released her and stepped back. Seconds later he turned and melted into the trees, leaving her trembling and alone with her thoughts.

As anxiety receded an icy hand of guilt clutched at her heartstrings. Anyone else would bask in Steele's love, feel fortunate to have such devotion from one so powerful and handsome.

Anyone wasn't her.

She let out a weary, resigned sigh. It was time to forget her human lover once and for all. She only wished, yet again, that she'd never left her son in his care.

She'd lost sleep wondering if maybe she could have protected her son, Pascal, even out here in the vast interior of Australia with the crude rules that governed the *Triskellon* gargoyles. The human world could be as harsh as the gargoyle edicts, undoubtedly more so by some of Saul's standards.

Guilt slid like toxin through her blood. Her "freedom of the skies" had been bought at great cost. Not only had she lost her only child, she'd given up the love of her life too.

Resolve steeled her spine as she began the long walk back to her *Triskellon* comrades. She'd made her choice, she'd have to live with that decision and push all regrets aside.

She shivered a little, and rubbed her arms. But she wasn't cold. Though Steele's obsession with her gnawed at her gut like an ulcer, he'd been much more to her than a lover. He'd become her protector, her guardian of sorts after he'd sought retribution in her honor when she'd been too emotionally overwrought to seek it herself.

But nothing could stop the panic attacks that had been left behind, a legacy of her assault.

She bit her lower lip. Yes, she should be counting her blessings Steele loved her, despite her failings as his heart-mate. As for her precious son, he would always be a tangible link to the lover she'd never forget.

A winged shadow flickered across the foliage above, circling a few times overhead until the gargoyle was all but skimming the treetops. Zahlee sucked in a breath. This aerial display was silent communication she was wanted. Urgently.

Chapter Two

Zahlee broke into a fast run, towards the direction of a small clearing just half a mile ahead. The gargoyle overhead would have little choice but to land there—the clearing she and Steele had used was too far away.

When she broke through the trees and into the grassy patch of land, Lolita, an elder of the *Triskellon* clan, was waiting, visibly impatient.

"There you are!"

Zahlee frowned. "What happened?"

"Not what. *Who.*"

Her frown deepened. "Lolita, what do you mean?"

The elder stepped forward, brushing back a silver-blonde lock of her hair. "Your son. He's come home."

Her thought processes went completely numb and then sped into double time. *Pascal was here*! Her pulse jerked as another thought took over. *Saul. Was he okay? Had her son come with bad news*?

She remained immobile for perhaps a millisecond. Then she spun around, taking off in a sprint to where her son awaited at the *Triskellon* camp.

Unable to use air currents—the gargoyle clan lived in deep caves high at the top of a mountain range—it took precious hours on foot before she finally arrived at the all too silent site that was cast in shadow, the sun drifting toward the far mountainous horizon.

Steele stepped forward from the cave she shared with him, carrying her clothes. His wings were high behind him, his emotions taut. "You got the news."

"Yes," she whispered. Her stomach churned with emotions she'd reined in all too long as she accepted her loose-fitting tunic and pants. She pulled them on, her wings snapping tight against her spine. "Pascal is home."

The *Triskellon* clan may have outwardly welcomed Pascal into their lives after he was born, but she'd been all too aware of the undercurrent of distrust toward her son. It had been the fundamental reason why she had left all those years ago.

The flesh-burning initiation, where the elders had seared *Triskellon* along Pascal's spine at the tender age of five, had been the last straw. Knowing he'd yet to face numerous gargoyle inductions that tested the males' strength, endurance and agility, she'd feared her half-human child wouldn't survive. She'd decided there and then that Pascal should experience life among humans, grow up without the pain and distrust he'd endured as a *Triskellon* member.

But she'd never intended to fall for a human, whose love for her, for a child who wasn't his own, was all exclusive, his adoration overflowing from an otherwise darkened soul.

In some ways, she understood the gargoyles distrust. Her son might have all the physical genetics of a gargoyle, but he did have a human father—and a depraved human at that.

It was no secret she'd been raped by a park ranger when she'd flown too far out of the *Triskellon* territory. She'd always held an innocent fascination toward humans, even before Saul. And when she'd seen a campfire, a large human hunched over a crude rotisserie of roasting wild rabbit, she hadn't thought about anything more than hiding her wings.

She'd shifted into human form and stepped naked toward the man.

When she'd stumbled back to the *Triskellon* camp days later, her bright-eyed innocence had been all but snuffed out, her soul darkened. Steele had taken one look at her and silently left to "take care" of her human rapist.

It had never been discussed again.

Steele nodded. "Tonight we celebrate Pascal's homecoming..." She closed her eyes, incredibly grateful and relieved by Steele's acceptance. "But now, it's my duty to send you back to your human lover."

Her lids flicked open, her eyes going wide. "What?"

"You are free to return to your human. I will take care of Pascal and his lover."

Her emotions went numb again even as her thoughts scrambled one after the other. *I won't get to see my son before I leave. I'll see Saul again soon. Pascal brought a lover—but surely not a human?*

No human would be tolerated here, not with the secrecy of the *Triskellon* clan.

"All I ask," Steele continued softly, decisively, "is that you stay with your human until his mortality ends, along with your obsession."

Sharp relief filled her, consumed her, even as desperation sucked at her soul. "I need some time with my son," she breathed. "Please, I haven't even seen him yet." She shook her head. "I can't go. I lost Pascal once, I won't lose him again."

Steele's face could have been carved out of the same rock as the humans' fairytale gargoyles. "You don't have a choice, not anymore. "

"Please, I—"

His wings snapped closed. "You'll have all the time you'll need with Pascal after your mortal is dead and buried."

So this was her punishment for not loving Steele? In the gargoyle world, Steele's word was law. Disobedience meant banishment, or worse.

Sorrow tore through her soul, hatred for the gargoyle leader bubbling up to the surface until even her eyes burned.

Bad enough that Steele had forced her to stay after she'd returned, never once allowing her to go back and see Pascal. Now he was forcing her to leave here—with the same outcome—never to see her son.

At least, not any time soon.

She lifted her chin. She wouldn't give him the satisfaction of being witness to her emotional carnage. Dragging in a breath, she mentally gathered every raw and bleeding sentiment back to where they belonged—away from Steele's shrewd, too arrogant stare.

Her heart iced over. Her voice came out like frost. "What about you?"

His eyes flared, hot and possessive. A muscle jerked to life in his set jaw. "I'll be here. And I'll be waiting."

Chapter Three

Two days later

Zahlee stilled beside the casino entrance, dry-mouthed, with her pulse jumping at the base of her throat. She'd wanted to stand out and be noticeable. Going by the admiring looks cast her way, she'd obviously achieved just that.

She smoothed a hand over the slinky, lime-colored dress cut on an angle, revealing more than it covered. One thigh was half bare, a shoulder and her delicate collarbone exposed.

She'd booked a modest hotel room using the bank account all the *Triskellon* members had access to, the same account from which she'd bought her dress and shoes. She'd washed and blow-dried her long hair into its naturally curly state—Saul had loved her wild hair—and now it swung almost to her waist as she sashayed inside, her stilettos tap-tapping across the marble floor.

She ignored the attention she drew as she moved through the casino, her thoughts now attuned to one thing. Saul.

Two men guarded the private elevator. She nodded to the older one. "Hello, Thomas."

He frowned for a moment, confusion written all over his swarthy face. "Zee, is that you?"

She smiled. Zee was the name Saul had used and it had stuck. "Who else?"

He shook his head, his stare openly roaming up and down her body. "You haven't changed one bit."

Yeah, immortality will do that.

"Thanks Thomas." She dipped her head toward the elevator. "If you don't mind."

"Let me call the boss first."

She shook her head. "No. I want to surprise him."

Thomas quirked a brow, his nut-brown eyes almost disappearing with his grin. "Oh, he'll be surprised all right. And you too, no doubt."

Don't count on it.

Thomas pressed the elevator button. As she stepped inside, she turned to him and said, "I never expected him to be a saint while I've been away. But I'm here now. There isn't any need for his other women."

Thomas saluted good luck as the glass doors swished shut and the elevator shot upward, stopping at the floor beneath the penthouse suite. It was here Saul conducted much of his business, legitimate and unlawful. What few people knew was that much of the profits here went to many different charities.

Her lips quirked. She'd often teased him privately about his secret Robin Hood status—taking from the rich to give to the poor. And he'd loved that she wasn't intimidated by him, that she said what she thought.

But suddenly she *was* intimidated. She wouldn't blame him if he despised her now.

A shiver slid up and down her spine. But she shook off further doubts as she stepped out of the glass elevator and onto the polished marble of a huge sitting room, where black leather recliners and a large entertainment unit took center stage.

She could hear the murmur of voices, the roar of excitement alongside low grumbles of disappointment. Saul and his men were in his private room, high-stakes gambling in progress.

She pushed open the wood-paneled door, viewing the scene before her. Cigar smoke billowed into the air, a haze of bluish purple surrounding the dozen or more men sitting around a large round card table, where hundred-dollar bills were piled high.

Saul had his back to her. A brunette languidly massaged his shoulders and a blonde leaned in close from a chair nearby.

Two women?

So this was the surprise Thomas had mentioned. Jealousy stabbed at her heart like an ice pick, then gave way to reluctant admiration. Saul always had been sexually dynamic, she'd not expect that to have changed just because she'd left.

One by one the men looked up at her, openly gawking. Saul's shoulders stiffened, despite the massage. It seemed he knew exactly who stood behind him even before he slowly turned to face her.

Her heart stilled as his intense, dark stare isolated her, drank her in. "Zee," he said huskily, almost uncertainly.

Love swelled from somewhere deep inside. "Saul," she whispered.

He stared at her for what seemed like an eternity. "You came back."

She took a half-step forward. Heat flooded through her body like a raging fever, flushing her skin with its warmth. Oh, god. Her feelings for him hadn't changed. Not one bit. She nodded. "Yes." She only wished she could have come sooner.

Her answer seemed to rouse him, to send him into action. "Everyone out," he said hoarsely. "Now!"

All the men except Lewie, his second-in-command, scattered, leaving behind their winnings. The women stayed put. The blonde threw Zahlee a poisonous glare but she was all honeyed sweetness when she turned back to Saul. "What about us, sweet cakes?"

He brushed her off and then shrugged free from the brunette's clasp on his shoulders. "Our business is done." He snapped his fingers to the much-older Lewie. "The girls are yours now. If they're willing," he warned.

Zahlee all but shuddered at the idea. Odds were, the girls would stay. They weren't about to give up their lavish lifestyle anytime soon. She only hoped the blonde and her brunette friend enjoyed rough sex. In the time, many years ago, when she'd been with Saul, she'd seen plenty of women bruised and sore from Lewie's sexual peccadilloes.

Lewie nodded, not bothering to hide the wicked gleam in his eyes as he ushered the women out.

Zahlee stepped away from the old thug. She was aware that age probably had not mellowed Lewie's sexual penchant for violence, and was even more aware that displaying anxiety would only invite his interest.

Saul stood then, tall and striking. He wasn't classically handsome but he possessed a powerful aura that drew the eye. Even now, so many years later, his whole persona screamed danger—perhaps more so. But it didn't repel. He was utterly charismatic.

He strode toward her. His brilliant gray eyes studied her, ate her up, as he clasped her hands and drew her farther into the room. "Tell me this time you're staying," he croaked.

Her breath caught. All these years later and he still really did love her, despite what she'd done. She'd hurt him so much, possibly even more than she'd hurt herself when she'd left him. Left her son. "I am."

Some of the tautness left his face as he nodded once. But determination as quickly set his face into tough, uncompromising lines. "Promise you won't leave again."

"I...yes. I promise."

His eyelids swept low, concealing his thoughts. His doubts? Then he leaned forward with a throaty growl, claiming her mouth with his.

Oh, Saul. She settled into the hard planes of his body, her mouth opening under his like a flower in full bloom. It'd been so long, too long.

Had he lain awake at night, every night, thinking about her? Had he touched himself, wishing it was she who touched him, wishing it was she who brought him to climax? Had he gone to sleep with her name on his mind, her face in his dreams?

Somehow she knew he had, in just the same way she had for him.

She couldn't withhold a moan as his tongue found and tangled with hers. He tasted of Cuban cigar smoke, whiskey and spices. She sighed, savoring his vitality, his maleness, even as the stubble on his jaw scraped over her delicate skin in a familiar caress.

No one else had ever made her feel like that. No one else had ever really made her feel. Period. She'd never connected with anyone emotionally, mentally, as she did with her human lover.

Saul's large hands cupped her ass, his fingers brushing up and down the slippery texture of her dress. He pulled back, his dark eyes alight with desire. "I never imagined lime green could look so damn good."

"You like?" she asked a little breathlessly.

"Oh, I like."

"Prove it," she whispered, holding his gaze and letting him know, really know what she wanted. And to hell with the consequences.

His breath hissed out. "Is that what you really want?"

"Yes." *Oh, yes.*

His hands tightened. "You do realize there's no going back now? No leaving me ever again?"

Chapter Four

At Zahlee's jerky nod, Saul did a half-turn then propelled her backward. He lifted her up onto the card table, his confined cock grinding against her damp panties.

She couldn't stop an urgent gasp as every nerve ending in her pussy, her clit, lit up in pleasure. She wished almost desperately that she hadn't worn underwear as she leaned back and twined her legs around his hips, the hem of her dress slipping to her hips.

His stare burned into her, hot and possessive. "Zee, I want you so much," he growled. "Damn it, I want to fuck you so good you'll never want another man but me."

"Then do it," she breathed.

Please!

His laugh was strained. "You never really were one for foreplay."

Bunching her panties in a white-knuckled grip, he wrenched the lacy material apart. With unsteady hands he unbuttoned his pants and jerked the zipper down, thrusting his boxer briefs down, along with his pants. Clasping the bunched dress at her hips he tugged her closer to the edge of the table and spread her wide.

Her throat dried at the sight of his engorged shaft, the head of his cock already glistening with pre-cum. She whimpered when he massaged her exposed clit with his hard, wet knob. "Fuck me," she said, her voice strangled. She wanted—needed—every inch of his big, thick cock inside her cunt.

She wanted to be connected to him, owned by him.

Triumph glinted in his stare when he rasped, "You know I love it when you talk dirty."

Then he slid inside her in one long stroke, her muscles sheathing him tightly, holding him in. She closed her eyes at the heady friction, the utter perfection of their joining.

How did I live without him for so long? I shouldn't have left.

Their breaths were heavy as they waited long seconds for her inner muscles to adjust. Saul was big, almost too big. But she'd been built for gargoyle lovers and even in human form her body was made for him.

With a groan Saul pulled out almost all the way. He plunged back inside her slippery pussy, the noisy, wet slapping sound as he began rocking in and out, a turn-on all its own.

She collapsed back onto the table, hundred-dollar notes wafting all around them and fluttering to the floor like expensive confetti. But she hardly noticed.

Her mind was attuned to the man who'd held a piece of her heart from the moment they'd met. She was linked to him in more than just the physical. Even after all these years their union was a meshing of two people who were meant to be, who were bound to one another.

He stilled just long enough to arrange her legs up over his torso, her feet resting behind his shoulders. His hot stare feasted on her exposed cunt, filled to capacity with his cock. He closed his eyes for a moment. A muscle flexed in his jaw. Then he rocked into her again, angling his cock so that it hit her G-spot dead center.

Holy shit!

She jackknifed on the table with a shrill gasp as an orgasm hit almost brutally. "Saul!" And this time she knew exactly whose name she called out as toe-curling shudders of bliss overtook her body.

Saul's face twisted with rapture as his seed exploded inside her in pulsing waves. Long seconds later, he released a slow, steadying breath, then smiled and said huskily, "Welcome back."

Her breath hitched as he slowly, deliberately withdrew his cock from her heat. She pushed up to her elbows, feeling sexy, slumberous and jubilant all at once. "Thank you." She cleared her throat. "That was most...unexpected."

Oh, she *had* hoped to seduce him, just not quite this soon.

He cupped her chin, pressing a warm, lingering kiss to her lips. "I'm sorry, of all the scenarios..." He shook his head. "I imagined so many times the perfect reunion when—if—I found you. But when Pascal disappeared too, I almost gave up hope."

Her heart plummeted, drowsy contentment instantly dissolving. She'd regained the love of her life but in doing so had lost the son she'd never really known. Her chest ached. Her throat felt thick. Tears formed, one sliding down her cheek before she could rein in her emotions.

Her only consolation was the fact Pascal would live eternally. She'd be able to make up at least some of the time she'd lost with him...after she lost Saul to his mortality.

Pain lanced through her heart at the thought. More tears threatened. Somehow she choked them back.

"Sweetheart, are you okay?" Saul murmured huskily, concern softening his stare. He blotted her tear with his thumb. "Is Pascal okay? Did he find you?"

She nodded, forcing a smile. "Yes, he found me." She swiped her face. "And he's fine. Though I...I never got to see him before I left."

"You didn't?" His eyes immediately hardened, glittering dangerously. But then he shook his head, dousing the fire. "I'm sorry. Enough of my questions. Pascal is alive and well and you're here with me. That's all I care about for now."

He tugged up his pants and boxer briefs before clasping her hands. "Come, let's take a shower and get some sleep. In the morning everything will make more sense."

She nodded, their footsteps echoing eerily as she walked unsteadily beside Saul out of the card room and toward the large bathroom with views to die for. "We are alone, aren't we?"

Saul chuckled at her question, though there was an underlying note of possessiveness to his voice that made her shiver and burn all at the same time. "We are, my love. I have you all to myself."

A spasm of lust created wet heat between her thighs. And as he led her across the bathroom's gleaming expanse of tiles her voice trembled only a little as she asked, "You don't use the penthouse suite anymore?"

"No. That is Pascal's." Flipping a lever, jets of hot water struck the white tiles below. He turned to her. "I keep it free for his return."

She bit her lower lip, nodding. "Thank you."

"Don't thank me," Saul half growled. "I consider him my son. When you left, he was the only spark in my otherwise dark world."

Oh, Saul. Guilt tore at her. "I never meant to hurt you, to hurt my son."

He nodded. "I know. I've had plenty of time to forgive you for leaving me. To accept that you are who you are. Keeping you from the skies was like asking an angel not to sing."

Tears again pricked her eyes. Saul did something to her beyond the physical. He made her feel things too long repressed.

He kissed her, gently, thoroughly, deeply. Then he was peeling her dress up and over her head and arms. She stood naked before him, luxuriating in the way his eyes feasted on her bare flesh, his stare heating her blood, her womb.

She stepped closer, dragging his tailored black jacket from his shoulders before unbuttoning his white dress shirt and discarding it too. When he stepped out of his pants and boxer briefs, she couldn't help but sigh with appreciation.

For a man just shy of his fiftieth birthday, he kept himself in peak physical condition. Lightly rippled abs, broad shoulders and powerful thighs revealed his love of the lap pool and the gym.

And lots of sex, a sly voice whispered.

She ignored the taunt—just. She hadn't exactly remained chaste since she'd left either. But now that she was back, it was as certain as night following day they'd remain true to one another.

Steam cocooned them in their own private world as they stared at one another, taking their fill.

Saul's cock jerked. He clearly liked what he saw too. He grinned, unabashed. "I think you've had enough cock for the moment." He gestured to the glass sliding doors. "After you."

She nodded, ignoring yet another ripple of lust that was somehow heightened by his restraint. But she was a little sore. Saul knew better than any that the size of his cock could only be taken in moderation.

Warmth drummed all around her as she stepped under the spray. Saul followed her inside the stall and she all but mewled in pleasure when his strong hands gently lathered her hair with vanilla-scented shampoo.

Her hair rinsed, she closed her eyes as he smoothed soap all over her body, like silk sliding over glass. Her skin shivered in response, her spine quivering at the sudden need to shift to gargoyle, to allow her wings to break out and wrap around them, keeping the rest of the world completely at bay.

The impulse weakened as she fought it. She was human now, for as long as she had to be. Like it or not, while she was with Saul, her gargoyle side had to be put away, forgotten. She came to him knowing to fully live in his world this time around she'd have to live her life as a human.

Never mind his insightful words about her needing the skies. Her love for him was strong enough to bear the sacrifice and stay grounded.

"Come," he said huskily, flipping off the water. "Let's get you dry."

She stood motionless as he dried her and she fought off waves of tiredness at his gentle strokes. Though fiercely independent as a gargoyle, there was something warm and fuzzy about letting this man take care of her.

After drying himself with the same fluffy bath sheet, he scooped her up into his arms and strode to the sitting room.

Moving into his large bedroom, he carried her to the bed and tucked her beneath crisp white sheets before pulling a soft, velvety bedcover up almost to her chin. "Sleep now," he said. "We'll talk some more tomorrow."

But tomorrow is your birthday. No words made it past her lips. Her eyes drifted closed and the shadows of sleep beckoned.

Chapter Five

Zahlee woke to the scent of breakfast and Saul's face creased into a pleased grin. "Good afternoon, sleepyhead."

Afternoon? She glanced through the wall of glass that was Saul's window. Late afternoon sunlight was losing its fight against the shadows outside, the tall city buildings looking dreary beneath the darkening overhead sky.

She sat up, the bedcovers falling to her waist. Her nipples pebbled under his hot gaze, her breasts growing heavy and hard. She swallowed past her dry throat. "I can't believe I slept for so long. Why didn't you wake me?"

"You evidently needed the rest."

When he placed the tray beside her on the bed, she noted his impeccable tuxedo, his neatly groomed salt-and-pepper hair. She put a hand to her mouth. Damn! She'd almost forgotten! "Happy birthday, Saul."

His grin deepened. Then he leaned in for a kiss, his mouth this time tasting of mint and exotic spices. She leaned into him on a sigh, savoring the moment. Savoring him.

When they finally moved apart, she said softly, "I'm sorry. I…I didn't get you anything."

"Are you kidding?" He curled a hand beneath her chin, his thumb tenderly tracing over her kiss-swollen lips. "You are the best present I could ever ask for."

Her heart stuttered. She'd left him. How could he possibly love her after she'd abandoned him all those years ago? Anguish tore at her. She didn't deserve him.

Her belly abruptly gurgled. He barked out a husky laugh then pronged some pancake, dripping with maple syrup, on a fork and lifted it to her lips. She opened her mouth and accepted his offering.

Had food ever tasted that good?

"Besides," Saul added huskily, "you know I'm the compulsive gift buyer. I've always enjoyed spoiling you."

There was no denying that. Saul had kept the gifts flowing almost on a daily basis. But in the end she hadn't thought twice about leaving them behind. Material possessions had been of no consequence in the bigger scheme of things. They couldn't heal a heart broken by having to give up the love of her life as a trade off for her freedom.

Couldn't heal her fractured soul by having to leave her son with the human race to protect him from the hardships and brutal inductions of the gargoyles.

His stare held hers as he fed her another mouthful. "Your clothes are all still here. I had them dry cleaned and stored away in the hope you..."

Would come back. The pancake was suddenly a tasteless lump clogging her throat.

He'd said when Pascal left he'd almost given up hope. Had he given up on her?

"Saul, please," she whispered, anguished. "I had no choice. I was dying here, suffocating. I had to be true to who I am. No matter how much it broke my heart."

And yours.

"And now you're here again. What's changed?" he asked.

"I..."

She closed her eyes. Would he even believe the truth? Accept that after she'd left him the *Triskellon* leader had forced her to stay away from Saul and her son all those years? The same gargoyle leader who'd become her lover and had then forced her to return to Saul until the human's demise?

Her eyes jerked open as Saul's fork clanked to the plate and he jackknifed to his feet, holding up a hand. "Don't," he said. "Just...don't. Don't try to explain. Don't try to make excuses. Don't try to make it right." He rubbed a hand over his face. "I can't hear this right now."

Shock held her silent. She'd never seen Saul so emotionally charged and teetering right on the edge of losing his tightly leashed control.

She searched his tortured gaze. Oh dear god. Despite her vow to stay, he thought he was going to lose her again. She could see it in his squared shoulders, his stiff stance and his not-quite-hidden grief. But instinct warned that no objection, however truthful, would assuage him right then.

"Okay," she breathed, forcing a neutral response. "I understand."

He unclenched his hands, letting out a long, slow breath. "I'm not sure that you do but thank you."

He turned to the window, taking a couple of strides to stare out at the cityscape below. He visibly relaxed. Once more in charge of his emotions, he pivoted to face her again. "A dinner birthday party and a show have been organized tonight. I'd like it if you'd accompany me."

She nodded. "Of course. I'd like that too."

His lashes swept low, his eyes a dark, dangerous glitter as he drank in her nakedness. Pain slashed across his features, as though he hated himself for wanting her.

Something squeezed inside her chest. He might want her, but he clearly trod a fine line between love and hate. She really had her work cut out for her to make him trust her again.

Her face must have given her away. He strode back to her, his expression fierce. "Zee, I hate that you left me, but I don't blame you for it. I know how you love to fly. I know you're free spirited." He let out a heavy breath. "I'm just... I'm not used to fighting myself, my feelings." At her nod he added huskily, "And honestly, I'm just so damn glad you're back, I can't find it in my heart to judge you."

She caught one of his hands in hers and placed in on her cheek. "I don't deserve you," she whispered.

When he started to protest she pressed a finger over his lips. Closing her eyes, she guided his hand downward, along her throat and the rise of one of her breasts. Her eyes snapped open as he cupped her there, his thumb scraping over her hardening nipple.

His hand dropped away and nothing but air caressed her tingling, aching breast. He shook his head, his eyes haunted. "You coming back to me—it's all I ever wanted. But now all I think about is how long we have together this time before you leave." Tension pulled his mouth into a hard line. "I'm not so sure I could live through that again."

"No. It's not like that. I'm never—"

He turned away, back rigid. "You'd better get ready."

She bit her tongue. He'd started with words of adoration and finished with dismissal. But she didn't blame him for the latter. She knew only that she couldn't make him believe her. This time her actions would have to speak for her.

He dragged a hand through his short, styled hair. "I've arranged something for you to wear. You'll find it hanging in the bathroom." He waved a hand toward the walk-in closet. "Everything else you'll find in there."

"Thank you."

He nodded once and then strode swiftly out of sight.

Minutes later, freshly showered, she was contemplating the crimson dress on its hanger before her. Its cut was elegant and simple, and she soon discovered, a perfect fit.

Saul had an amazing flair for fashion. Always had. She twirled before the full-length mirror, the spliced, multi-layered hem floating outward like a fairy dress.

Saul had a flair for everything.

Back in the bedroom, she walked to the closet and discovered all her old clothes hanging neatly. Most were ageless, classic styles that could be worn any decade. Dozens of shoes lined custom-made shoe racks. She selected and donned a delicate Egyptian-style pair of shoes, their long straps encircling her calves.

She cast her eyes over the shelves of lacy underwear. She stepped back. This time, she'd do without.

She heard Saul's tread behind her and turned to face him. He raised a dark eyebrow, his admiring gaze sweeping her up and down. "You're beautiful."

"Thank you." She cleared her throat. "Am I forgiven then?"

He let out a sigh. "Of course, Zee. You must know I act like all kinds of foolish when it comes to you." He stepped forward and said huskily, "Turn around."

She twisted obediently, her back to him. He lifted her heavy hair aside, his warm lips brushing the sensitive skin along her nape. She shivered with longing, with deep need. Then his mouth moved away, replaced by the cool touch of an expensive gold chain. A heavy diamond pendant settled between her breasts.

"Saul, you don't need to—"

"It's my birthday, indulge me. And it pleases me to spoil you."

She nodded but suddenly the beautiful chain felt like a leash, a noose that—if she let it—would slowly, inexorably tighten, choking her freedom right out of her.

She stemmed the dangerous sensations, banished the anxiety that had reared its head, if only for a moment. The freedom she'd once been so desperate to attain hadn't been anywhere near as wonderful as she'd imagined it would.

Oh, she'd gotten her freedom of the skies all right, but the freedom to leave the *Triskellon* clan without consequences had been taken much away from her. Steele had seen to that.

His mouth brushed her scalp, his breath warm as his lips lingered. "My party awaits, we'd better go."

Chapter Six

All eyes turned their way as Saul escorted her into the Casino's showroom on the fourth floor. The scattering of round tables had been removed. One huge rectangular table was set close to the stage and covered by a snowy-white cloth, trios of flickering, silver candles adorning the middle.

A man played a baby grand on a small stage set in a corner of the room, away from the curtained main stage. Drinks waiters appeared from a side door, bottles of chilled champagne and cold bottled beer held aloft on trays.

Lewie stood, his chair scraping back. "Happy birthday, boss."

A chorus of *happy birthdays* ensued, a good thirty or forty men and women coming to their feet and madly clapping.

"Another year alive," one of Saul's men announced loudly. "Congratulations."

Saul grinned, tugging her even closer to his side. "With my many enemies, every year I'm not in a pine box is a bonus."

Zahlee kept the tsunami wave of shudders all on the inside. Even so, she couldn't stop the chill that slid up and down her spine from spiking her skin with goose bumps.

Just the thought of Saul not being around made her feel hollow inside. And not for the first time, she wondered how it would feel to be an ordinary human, growing old with Saul, sharing each other's pain, each other's joy. Each other's milestones.

Lewie strode forward and Zahlee stepped aside as he gave Saul an affectionate bear hug, slapping his back. He turned to her next, his stare lingering on her a little too long. "You look amazing."

"Thank you." The words were forced and they both knew it.

Saul speared Lewie with a look that made Zahlee think alpha, and then he was leading her to the table and pulling out her seat. No sooner had he sat beside her than the first course arrived, like clockwork.

While Lewie's two women ate delicately and sparingly—and no doubt the handful of other women at the table—she all but wolfed down each course, appreciating every morsel of the seafood ravioli, whole stuffed quail with Greek side salad, and finally a rich chocolate fondant.

Though she was in human form, she still carried all her gargoyle characteristics. Her DNA demanded sustenance to keep her going, to produce the ability to shift into gargoyle and back to human at any time.

Lewie's blonde and brunette duo exchanged a look and then openly sniggered.

Zahlee raised her chin then slowly, deliberately, licked each of her fingers free of chocolate, like a satisfied woman after a good lovemaking session.

Saul's rumble of laughter filled the air. He tilted her chin up with a thumb and said approvingly, "I always did love your healthy appetite, my sweet."

The smile she exchanged with him was secretive, seductive. His eyes glowed in response, primitive and hot. And she realized he now paid the price for his earlier ardent restraint.

The lights abruptly dimmed. The man at the piano was joined by a trumpet player and a saxophonist. A few seconds later the room was filled with a happy birthday tune just as a spotlight hit the stage and a buxom redhead stepped through the curtains.

Zahlee arched a brow as the woman on stage fixed her sultry stare on Saul and sang her rendition in a sexy, come-hither voice.

The song finally over, the jazz band fired up a raunchy tune, which allowed the redhead to drop any pretence of modesty as she strutted around the stage. She slipped free from her sequined jacket and barely there, ass-covering skirt, to reveal a glittery white bra and G-string.

Zahlee squirmed in her seat. She was aware that Saul's eyes had barely strayed to the redhead. His stare had remained on her like a predator waiting for a reaction, even as the men around the table roared approval, their eyes wholly focused on the stripper on stage.

The dancer stepped off the stage and onto the big table. And though she stuck a thumb in her mouth to project schoolgirl innocence, her gyrations and hungry eyes suggested nothing short of a come-eat-me look.

Zahlee swallowed, despising the woman and yet unable to look away.

The appreciative male roars grew in volume as the stripper unclipped her scanty bra and her large breasts spilled free. A bellybutton ring flashed like fire under the dazzling light as she cupped her breasts, fondling them.

The dancer smiled suggestively, pushing a hand down the front of her G-string to touch herself, her stare not once leaving Saul.

Zahlee grew hot, aroused despite herself. Then again, what did she expect with her gargoyle genetics? She was hardwired to be stimulated easily, to breed and repopulate her dwindling species.

It never ceased to amaze her that a human she'd hated had managed to impregnate her when no gargoyle ever had. Her only wish was that the one human she truly loved was Pascal's real father—a stupid and perhaps selfish wish, knowing that Saul did love Pascal like his own son. When she at last turned to meet Saul's eyes, she witnessed his disinterest in the dancer who all but fucked him from afar. But then she noted the gleam behind his stare, a zealous appetite for her whetted by the exotic dancer.

Zahlee smiled, her lashes dropping low as her pussy tightened with anticipation.

It was going to be a long night.

The stripper, miffed by Saul's rejection, turned away from them to find the next best thing—apparently Lewie. The redhead stood above his lustful stare with her legs spread wide apart. Her hands moved to cup behind her head, her large breasts jutting out even further as she closed her eyes.

Lewie whipped her G-string aside, exposing her pussy with its strip of red curls. And without ceremony he thrust four of his fingers into her channel, his hand moving with rhythmic, forceful expertise.

Saul waved at the jazz band to stop. As they dispersed, Zahlee watched Lewie scrape a thumb over the stripper's clit with unrelenting, bulldozer pressure. The woman moaned, a sound of pained relief, her cunt juices smearing her thighs.

Lewie's wicked, carnal gaze slid over to Zahlee for the briefest moment, then moved on to the ladies seated on either side of him as he dropped his hand.

Zahlee shivered. The redhead might suffer from humiliation right then but the blonde and brunette would be bruised, sore and hard-core fucked come morning.

The stripper's high-heeled shoes clacked across the table in the ensuing thick silence. Once back on stage, the redhead scooted behind the curtains without a backward look.

Saul cast Lewie a dark look. "I hope you've all enjoyed tonight's entertainment." He twisted back to Zahlee. "Zee, if Lewie offended—"

She sent Lewie a scathing look. "Actually, he did." Repressed emotions bubbled to the surface, scalding heat flushing her face. "And I think he should be made to suffer the consequences of his actions."

Chapter Seven

Saul ignored the audible gasp from the people around the table. He leaned forward, brushing the back of his fingertips along her jaw. "Oh?"

She nodded, her hands squeezing into fists on her lap. "He's a monster who gets kicks out of demeaning women."

Saul raised a brow. "Then what would you suggest as his penalty?"

She lifted her chin. "No women. No sex. For a month."

Lewie pushed to his feet, his face mottled with purple and red. "That's outrageous. Boss, you can't possibly take her seriously—"

Saul stood without a word but there was steel in his stare as he faced the other man down. Lewie dropped back to his seat with a savage oath and Saul gestured to the blonde and brunette. Seconds later they were tripping over themselves to find the quickest exit.

Saul turned his stare on each individual around the table. "I expect each one of you to monitor Lewie's movements. If for some reason he ignores the punishment, the first person to inform me will be amply rewarded. "

Rage shimmered from Lewie like fire radiating heat. Lewie would undoubtedly want to exact his own brand of revenge on her. Zahlee held his hard stare and smiled. She'd not be intimidated. Not this time. Not by any man.

With a satisfied nod Saul sat and took her hand in his.

Thank you, she mouthed.

He leaned forward and tugged her toward him until they met halfway. "You're welcome, my angel," he murmured.

Their lips gently touched. He groaned a little and the pressure intensified. Her mouth parted as the tip of his tongue slid inside, flooding nerve endings with heat. Lost in the moment she sighed, opening her mouth fully to his skilled seduction.

A chair scraped back loudly. They pulled apart, dazed.

She realized Lewie was standing, waiting for their attention, the other guests struck silent by his nerve. "The dinner and show is over now, boss. Can I suggest the men withdraw for cigars and a scotch?"

Saul stared hard at Lewie. The other man's gaze dropped once again and Saul returned his full attention to Zee. Few would be fooled. Lewie had received a temporary reprieve but he'd pay for his disrespect.

Saul waved a hand through the air, letting his wrath slide for the moment. "You men can go. I'm staying with my woman."

The silence stretched, taut and expectant. She glanced at the shocked faces around them, most of them familiar. Had they forgotten how smitten Saul had been with her all those years ago? She had been his everything.

Yes, and you were stifled.

The room seemed suddenly to shrink, the people sitting too close, the heavy feminine perfumes, the cigar smoke, too cloying, too smothering. Her spine tingled and itched with the sudden inner upheaval, her wings ready to burst free.

She closed her eyes, breathing slowly, controlling her panic. The violent sexual assault from her past may have made her susceptible to these occasional, terrifying bouts of anxiety, but she'd learned how to overcome them.

"Sweetheart, are you okay."

She opened her eyes, forcing composure. "I'm fine." She swallowed hard then managed a smile. "You go on up with the men. I...I'd like some fresh air."

His eyes darkened fractionally. She held her breath, her teeth gnawing on the inside of one cheek. Then he relented with a sharp nod. "Very well."

But it wasn't very well. She sensed his reluctance, his desire to stay by her side.

The women ordered coffee and tea as the men scraped back their chairs and moved toward the elevator that would take them to the private card room. Ever the gentleman, Saul pulled out her chair first, so that she too could leave the room.

She nodded and then made her escape toward the glazed doors leading to the large balcony. She felt the women's stares on her back, had a pretty good idea she'd be their topic of conversation when the gleeful gossip about the stripper and Lewie had palled.

She sucked in the outside air. Unlike the fresh purity of the inland air, it was tainted with pollution, an amalgam of city fumes. Even so, she was grateful for the space, the solitude and relative peace and quiet.

She hooked her hands over the rail. Moonlight flooded her face, a cool breeze whispered over her skin. She squeezed her eyes shut. For one moment at least she could pretend there wasn't a blanket of city lights spread out before her, pretend she wasn't sharing this cityscape with over four and a half-million people.

She let out a soft sigh, imagining then she was flying, the wind pushing beneath her wings as she soared ever upward, without a care in the world. Except, she'd never really been guilt free—even in flight she had agonized over Saul and the son she'd left behind.

Was Pascal okay? Her heart wrenched. Did he wonder—again—why she had left him, wonder if she even loved him? Did he even know she'd been given no choice but to leave the moment he'd arrived at the *Triskellon* camp?

Her teeth bit into her lower lip and she tasted the coppery tang of blood, the saltiness of her tears spilling down her cheeks.

She had no idea what her son looked like. She had no clue even to how he'd turned out as an adult, living all those years with Saul.

A strangled laugh pushed past her lips. She'd been such a fool! No child deserved to grow up without a mother, no matter how harsh the environment. A mother's love was everything.

It had almost killed her to leave Pascal behind. But that one year they had been with Saul and all his human friends had made him so happy. He'd beamed whenever Saul had so much as looked his way.

Damn it! He'd fit so well into the human world she hadn't wanted to tear him away.

She'd thought she'd given her young son the ultimate sacrifice by not uprooting him from everything and everyone he loved to bring him back to the distrustful stares of the gargoyle clan. Back to the very people they'd fled.

She sighed, aching to see her son.

Saul had clearly loved him, she'd known that, but she realized now that obstacles could be overcome. Fear could be turned into courage, weakness into strength. She'd learned that and more firsthand after the father of Pascal had planted his seed in her unwilling body.

She'd kept all her fears, all her self-doubts on the inside. Then she'd met Saul all those years ago and her every doubt had dissolved. Nothing and no one could touch her. No one would be game to cross the mobster boss.

It was only when she'd left Saul that everything had started to fall apart, the anxiety attacks returning with a vengeance.

She sensed Saul behind her a nanosecond before she heard his tread. But she didn't turn to him and ask what he was doing out here with her instead of sharing scotch and cigars with the men.

She remained motionless as every nerve ending screamed for him, for his skilled touch. Then his hands clasped her waist as though they belonged there. On the softest of sighs she leaned into him, giving in to her desire and soaking up his heat, his strength, his vitality.

I love him so much.

His lips trailed over the side of her throat as his big, capable hands moved to her front and slipped low. Using a slow, circular motion he massaged her pussy through the slippery fabric of her dress until she was almost a puddle at his feet and craving so much more.

Oh god. How did he do it? How did he leave her wanting him so badly? How did he help her forget the past until she lived only for the moment? How did the need to soar through the skies become nothing short of an afterthought?

"You're not wearing underwear." He growled in her ear, sending a cascade of goose bumps over her body. She managed a nod and his breath was warm on her earlobe as he asked, "What are you doing out here? I mean, really doing?"

She tensed. A smattering of high-pitched laughter floated their way, the women's gossip obviously in full swing.

"Let me guess," he said into the silence, "you wish you were flying right now?"

"Yes...I was," she conceded weakly, barely thinking straight.

His hands tightened. "Is there anything I can do to make you forget that idea?"

She could feel his cock straining against his pants and her breath hissed when he ground his shaft between her thighs. "Yes," she said hoarsely.

Oh, yes!

His breath became heavier in her ear when one of his hands moved and she heard the whistle of his zipper coming undone, the rustle of his pants and boxer briefs. He tugged up the hem of her dress. His freed cock pushed insistently against her bare ass.

"Someone might see us," she said weakly, titillated and appalled in equal measure.

"Yes, they might. Isn't that a delicious thought?"

She threw her head back, allowing him to suckle the sensitive curve of her throat as she gasped, "You. Always. Did. Thrive. On. Danger."

It was just one of the many things she loved about him.

"I could hardly be in the position I'm in without enjoying some danger."

Touché.

He lifted her hem a little higher. A growl rumbled from deep in his chest when he spread her thighs with a knee and rasped, "You feed on danger just as much as I."

Then he thrust forward, deep into her eager cunt.

"Oh, Saul."

His cock filled her with a pain she barely acknowledged as pleasure immediately followed. He drew back then drove forward again. And again. Hard and fast. No foreplay and very little restraint. Just a wild, utter abandonment that excited the gargoyle in her and turned her human side on in oh so many ways.

Growing pleasure was spearheading too quickly toward orgasm.

And he knew it.

Her dress no longer a barrier, he deftly parted her vulva with one hand and massaged her clit. The act pushed her doubly quick to the edge of climax and beyond and she shattered around him with a startled cry, clinging to the railing with a white-knuckled grip.

He plunged deeper still, his outspread hands clasping her hips to drag her back against him. He groaned, long and hard, holding her in place over his erupting cock.

They stayed joined for some minutes, panting and still. Then Saul reluctantly pulled free. He settled her dress back into place before refastening his pants. Clasping her forearms, he turned her gently to face him. "You're safe. No one saw."

"Yes." Her legs barely supported her with the lethargic aftereffect of great sex. "But your friends must be wondering where you are."

He dropped his hands, his grin wickedly amused. "Oh, I think they have a fair idea."

No doubt.

She swayed a little and he took hold of her again. Staking claim? He studied her face. "Are you okay?"

"Yes." She nodded. "Yes, of course. I'm just...tired. I probably should have an early night." Some time alone to think, to adjust.

"Sounds like a fine idea. I'll just let the guests know we're retiring early."

"No. Please. Stay with your friends."

His shadowed eyes glittered. "You don't want my company?"

"It's not like that—well, not entirely. Your men already dislike me, knowing I left you, especially Lewie. And now...after my request, I don't want to give any one of them even more ammunition."

Saul's rage was tangible. "Lewie is more than aware I'd kill him if he so much as touched a hair on your head. You know that."

Tell him! A voice screamed inside her head. *Tell him the fears you still carry around after all these years, the panic attacks that strike you when you least expect them. The deep-seated foreboding you feel whenever someone like Lewie so much as looks your way.*

She couldn't tell him. The words simply couldn't push past the sudden thickness in her throat. And somehow it felt too late to tell him now.

Way too late.

Though it had been years after the rape incident when she'd met Saul, the memory and grief had still been too fresh, too raw to confide in him. No matter how naïve and innocent she'd been at the time, somehow she'd felt guilty—still felt guilty—as though she'd asked for everything she'd gotten by approaching her would-be attacker in all her naked glory.

And deep down, she couldn't help but wonder just what Saul would think and say if she told him.

At her silence, one of his hands gripped her chin, forcing her gaze back toward his too-astute stare. She swallowed. He all but quivered with suppressed emotion, with bleak despair.

"What is this really about?" His voice roughened. "Are you already pining for your old life? Your freedom? Your...lover?" He bit the last word out as if it was hot acid on his tongue.

"No, not my lover. But yes, to my freedom. Surely you can understand? I've had the liberty of the skies for so long now—"

His grip tightened almost painfully. "No flying. No wings." His silky quiet voice throbbed with danger. "Promise me."

Chapter Eight

"No." Her answer shocked even her. It wasn't until that moment that she knew it was an impossible request, despite her earlier thoughts to the contrary. "I am a gargoyle. You can't take that away from me. No one can."

His hands dropped. He shook his head. "You're right. Of course you're right, I know that." He moved back, releasing a jagged breath. "What was I thinking?"

She followed him and took hold of his arm. Sometimes the best defense was direct attack. And she really, really wanted to attack him right then, make him pay for wanting to take away her only escape from the terrible memories haunting her every single day. "Why don't you tell me, Saul? What were you thinking?"

He shook his head. "Bloody hell, Zee. Don't you see? I don't want to lose you. Not again." His eyes closed, concealing his pain. "But your fierce independence, your free spirit, it's a big part of you and I can't change that. I don't want to change that!"

Her fingers tightened on his arm, squeezing the taut muscle. "Trussing me up with rules is what pushed me away the first time."

He nodded, releasing a heavy breath. "I know." He grinned ruefully. "Mortal rules don't apply to you. They never have. You're no one's puppet." The hand he moved to cup beneath her chin was all gentle tenderness this time. "I can't believe I just tried to change that."

She released a sigh, tension ebbing. Everything was going to be all right.

"Come on," he said, taking her hand in his. "Let's dance."

"But your men are waiting."

"It's my party, my birthday. And I want to spend it with you."

He drew her back into the showroom they'd vacated. The women were still there, drinking their coffee and tea, a couple of them tossing back champagne in slender flutes. Their eyes went wide as Saul walked her out onto the polished wooden floor that occasionally served as a dance floor.

He pulled her into his arms, nodding at the man who'd returned to play piano. A dreamy, romantic piece filled the room, at complete odds with the women's stares that cut into her back like hot blades.

"We've got a rapt audience," she said with an arched brow.

"Mmm. Every single one of them is wishing they were you."

Yes. They each want to be the woman in your arms. Her laugh was half hysterical. "Not if they saw the gargoyle side of me."

He pulled his head back. "You look nothing like those gargoyle statues that guard cathedrals. You hardly change at all in your winged form."

True. Except for a thickening of her spine and her huge wings, there wasn't a lot of visible change, despite the tales to the contrary.

"You don't like me as a gargoyle." Funny, having said it aloud, bitter emotions immediately churned within, her vision swimming with the threat of tears.

His nostrils flared. "I love you in any form. What I despise is the fact your wings, your love of flying, means I may one day lose you."

She closed her eyes for a moment, letting him expertly guide her around the floor as she said, "I've only ever wanted to enjoy the best of both worlds—no judgments, no recriminations."

His brow furrowed and his stare was thoughtful. "Sweetheart, do you think such a thing is even possible?"

"Yes. Yes, I do."

His hands slid over the curve of her ass cheeks. He wedged her close and a little mewl of need escaped her lips. Her stilettos provided just enough height for the restrained bulge of his cock to push almost dead center against her pussy.

"So you want your cake and to eat it too?" he murmured, the serious note in his voice revealing acceptance of the idea.

"Is that so wrong?"

He clasped her hands as she leaned backward in a half-sweep, his cock jutting hard against her pussy before he pulled her upright again. One of his hands moved to cup behind her head. He held her stare. "No, it's not wrong. It's who you are."

Thank you. "Saul, I'm here to stay this time, no matter what form I take."

They stilled, caught up in each other's stare. The piano tinkled on.

"You really are," he murmured at last, his relief palpable.

She nodded. "I made a promise. I'm not leaving you Saul. Not ever again."

His eyes were fierce. Possessive. And yet tenderness shone deeper still. "I believe you."

She nodded, her chest aching. Compared to her immortal years, she had only a short time with Saul. She didn't want to waste even a second of that precious time on distrust and suspicion.

"Let's get out of here," Saul said thickly.

In an almost dreamlike daze, she followed him into the elevator and rode it up to his floor, ever aware of the growing heat between them, the anticipation. The utter need.

When they stepped into the suite, the rowdy crowd of men could easily be heard in his private card room. She glanced at Saul.

He grinned. "Seems they're managing to celebrate without me just fine."

"Should we wait until they've—"

"No. They know better than to invade any part of my private living space."

She gasped, pressing a hand to her mouth as a sudden memory tweaked.

Saul frowned. "Sweetheart, what's wrong?"

"I left my underwear in the card room."

Amusement at her modest concern lurked just beneath his heated stare. "I have a very discreet cleaning service. You have absolutely nothing to worry about."

She slumped, so utterly relieved. It was probably beyond weird to strip and fly naked in front of any member of her clan without any self-consciousness, yet be so ill-at-ease with just the thought of her torn panties on the floor for anyone to see. For the perverted Lewie to eyeball.

Saul led her into his huge bedroom. Closing the door behind them with a firm click, he had her stand in front of a full-length mirror that was opposite the floor-to-ceiling window.

"You don't see your beauty, do you?" he asked huskily. "I mean, not really."

Gargoyles were genetically a beautiful species, but they didn't view themselves the way humans did. There was no artifice to them in either form, they embraced their natural beauty, loved themselves for who they were and appreciated their wings for the gift of flight, despite the fact humans would consider the webbed, batlike wings ugly.

A human's vanity was one of the reasons a gargoyle was unwilling to live permanently as human and sacrifice the utter joy of flight.

She frowned, peering at the mirror. If she looked, really looked, at herself through human eyes, she could see why men approved.

Her long dark hair with its wild curls framed her oval face, enhancing large hazel eyes and her just-kissed lips that bordered plump. She wasn't tall for her species. In her heels she was a few inches shorter than Saul, who was just shy of six feet.

Saul cocked his head to the side, studying their reflection. "I can't help but wonder what you see in me," he mused aloud.

He wasn't classically handsome. He was rugged, built like a professional football player after a lot of knocks. His nose was a little crooked, a touch big, his jaw a little too square, his stare a little too hard. But add the power almost bristling from him and the entire package drew the eye, made him charismatic as hell.

She arched a black brow. "You've never been short of female admirers." She lifted her hands, covering his fingers clasped at her waist. Her skin was porcelain smooth alongside his dark, rough-textured hands, her long fingers comparatively slender and dainty. "I like you just exactly how you are."

"Like?" he murmured. "I was hoping for a little more than that."

He wasn't just talking about his looks and they both knew it. But she wasn't ready just yet to say those three little words that had filled her head from almost the moment she'd laid eyes on him all those years ago.

She guessed she still had trust issues to deal with when it came to the human race...to human men. Her attacker—Pascal's father—really had scarred her emotionally and mentally, for life.

She shivered, but resisted an urge to jerk out of Saul's arms. She had to tell him the truth about her past if they had any real hope of a future together.

"Guess I'll just have to convince you, hmm?" he said into the silence. Turning her in his arms, his eyes searching hers, he whispered huskily, "I. Love. You."

Chapter Nine

Oh, Saul. I love you too.

The words built in Zahlee's throat. Then Pascal's mouth abruptly slanted over hers. She collapsed against him on a moan, once again caught up in the moment until all else but the now was a distant memory.

But there was no great urgency. This time they took their time to rediscover one another, their tongues tangling and tasting in a leisurely exploration that was like a well-loved journey travelled all over again.

He pulled back, his expression tender and fierce all at once as he pushed the sleeves of her dress off her shoulders. He watched, clearly fascinated as it fell in a whisper of sound to the floor, barely skimming her naked body.

He released a ragged breath, drinking her in. "I envy Pascal his artistic ability right now."

"He's an artist?" she asked breathlessly, drinking in the knowledge even as she drank in the man before her. God, she'd have done anything to come back and see her son, spied on him from afar if need be. Anything just to know he was happy, safe.

Yes. A sculptor." Saul gently clasped either side of her jaw, drawing her close as he stared at her with an intense, primal hunger. "I'd give almost anything to have his talent, to capture exactly how you look with nothing on but your pendant."

Her smile wobbled a little as Saul's thumbs trailed across her lips.

"Zee." His stare darkened and with a primal growl he took her mouth once more.

Heat surged deep inside and radiated outward until she wondered if it was lava, not blood that ran through her veins, that gathered in the core of her pussy and burned with wanton need.

Mouths still joined, she pushed his jacket over his shoulders, dragging it from him before unbuttoning his shirt with unsteady

kissed the instep of her foot, trailing kisses along her heel and past her ankle, his tongue swirling as he worked his way down her calf and along the hypersensitive skin of her inner thigh.

Her breath caught when he parted her legs. His head dipped. Oh god. Fire tore through her body and gathered deep in her womb. She jerked as his tongue flicked the hard nub of her clit, his teeth then gently scraping the sensitized flesh.

She looked down at his dark head between her legs. It was almost as erotic as the act itself. Almost. Her spine arched. She panted for breath. His tongue swirled and flicked, creating electric, pulsating flashes that rendered her almost insensible.

He spread her wider, his tongue relentless. Her mouth dropped open, making soundless noises at the exquisite sensations he created. His teeth again scraped the hard nub of her cunt. And when a tidal wave of delight coursed through her body, she couldn't hold back a long cry of ecstasy.

He looked up from her drenched pussy, smiling with triumph. His eyes glittered. "Do you know how utterly beautiful you are when you come?"

"No. Not without a mirror," she joked weakly, raising a hand before letting it flop back to the bed.

His stare narrowed, a wicked smile twitching his lips as he released her legs and crawled over her to straddle her. "What a splendid idea, my love."

She frowned, her belly twisting. "What...do you mean?"

His grin widened, the grooves in his brow deepening. He climbed off the bed and leaned down to take her into his arms. He slowly lowered her to her feet beside the bed. They stood sideward to a full-length mirror.

She closed her eyes to the sensation of skin against skin, heat against heat. Her nipples scraped his lightly haired chest, his cock grazing the flesh of her belly.

She stumbled, weak kneed. Her eyes jerked open. Saul's hands moved to rest on her shoulders. His smile all alpha, he twisted her around so she faced the bed.

"Now you can watch yourself climax," he murmured throatily. "See what I see when you fall apart."

His cock nudged between her thighs. She spread her legs apart with an eager sigh and bent from the waist, aware that in this position she was every bit the omega. And Saul—he was alpha through and through.

"Look at us," he commanded throatily.

She turned her head just as his cock pushed into her slick, wet heat. *Oh sweet heaven.*

His strong thighs were jammed tight to the rounded globes of her ass. She quivered when his hands moved, fondling her breasts and tight nipples. He rocked inside her with fierce strokes, causing fire to lick through her cunt at the delicious friction, at the carnal image she couldn't tear her eyes away from.

"Saul!" She came with a suddenness that took her breath away, her muscles locking onto his cock as it erupted seconds after.

His stare caught and held hers in the mirror. "As you can see, we're perfect for each other."

Chapter Ten

In the oldest denim jeans she'd been able to find and a rose-pink blouse unbuttoned at the throat to reveal glimpses of the pendant beneath, Zahlee had never felt more beautiful. She hadn't glowed in her pregnancy all those years ago, but at least now she understood the term.

Being with Saul, having him make love to her, she was blossoming again, like a rosebud opening to the sun.

She turned in the passenger seat of the SUV, drawn helplessly to Saul.

His profile with the darker shade of growth along his jaw added to his harsh, sinfully dangerous aura. He was in superb shape for a man of his mortal age. Yes, he'd lived a lot in his years—the tough edge of his lifestyle, the suffering and adversity was clear in his rough-hewn features, his shrewd eyes. But despite all that, he looked to be in his prime.

"You said you wanted to surprise me," she said. "I think I'm already surprised by the fact you're taking the SUV out for a drive."

He had quite a collection of luxury vehicles in the private, underground parking area of the casino. But aside from a couple of his favorite sports cars he took for an occasional run, he more often than not rode in the back of his stretch limousine, where many a deal had been sealed on a handshake with a business associate.

"Oh, I think my surprise is a little bit more exciting than the car I'm driving," he teased, a smile twitching the corners of his lips and totally wiping away his hard-edged expression.

"In that case," she said, reaching to select a rosy-red apple from the picnic basket on the back seat, "I might as well enjoy the ride."

Saul's smile widened, his eyes glinting at the double meaning. "Please do."

Curiosity about his surprise burned through her mind as she bit into her apple. As she crunched around her mouthful, Saul broke into a husky chuckle.

At her abstracted frown he murmured, "I can't help but love everything you do. Even the most mundane things like your healthy appetite." He took her hand for a moment and squeezed. "I guess that's true love, hmm?"

Her throat constricted and she had to forcibly swallow. "How could you possibly love me after everything I've done?"

To you and to my son.

"Despite my stupid demand that you not fly, I knew who—what—you were, from almost the very beginning."

So he had. There had been instant chemistry between them from their very first eye contact at a cabaret show in the casino. They had been at separate tables near the stage, but with their chairs almost touching back-to-back. He'd started a conversation that had seen them turn their chairs ever outward until they'd been facing each other.

She hadn't remembered one minute of the show and yet Saul's every word had been seared into her brain. She hadn't been able to resist him, hadn't been able to decline his invitation to go out the next night, when he'd taken her to the very same show.

He hadn't wanted her to miss it a second time.

She'd fallen for him. Hard. And in that second night after the show, before they'd even made love for the first time, she'd opened up and told him all her secrets—except one. And just like that he'd believed her. Accepted her. Wanted her, despite her differences or perhaps even a little because of them.

She'd discovered Saul's deeper side, his adoration a quality few people ever saw. And she'd thrown it all back in his face the day she'd left him.

Saul ran an outspread hand through his hair. "I have to admit there are times, even now, I feel a burning anger take hold, but I'm just too damn thankful you've come back for any of those feelings to last."

"I'm glad." Even more so because of the fact that she knew love and forgiveness had never been high on Saul's list of priorities. He hadn't become wealthy and successful by being soft, romantic and kind.

She turned to look out the windshield when he slowed and flipped on the indicator, turning off the highway onto a dirt road. A sign read Big Tree Heights and then they were cruising along the gentle rise of a narrow lane with eucalyptus trees towering along either side.

She opened the window and breathed in the invigorating, crisp country air. Twenty minutes later Saul turned onto another road, this one rough and uninviting. He slowed again as a large metal gate came into view. "Private property" was emblazoned in large print across a sign on the gate.

Retrieving a remote from the SUV's console, he pushed a button so that the huge gates swung inward from their posts. As they drove through Zahlee noted the seemingly endless, high chain-wire fence that enclosed the property.

She arched a brow. "We're visiting someone? Is that the surprise?"

He laughed. "Not even close."

With the gates closing behind them, the road ahead inclined sharply. The SUV lurched over the rocky, potholed road, but Saul drove with a confidence that mirrored his personality, tackling the near-vertical rise that made her giddy with an adrenaline she realized she'd missed.

He slowed as a large adult goanna, a couple of meters in length, ambled across the road in front of them, its reptilian forked tongue flicking in and out. It turned its mottled black and gray head toward them, assessing the danger. An instant later it took off running, using its sharp claws to climb the nearest paperbark tree with effortless ease.

Zahlee clutched at the overhead hand grip as Saul accelerated again. "I believe you, we're not visiting anyone. No human I know would choose to live out here."

Her mouth snapped shut. Her eyes went wide. A three-story house reared up at the top of a summit ahead, almost as though it was a part of the mountain. Sunlight gleamed against its huge tinted windows, the valley of trees that fell away from the driveway its extended front yard.

"Wow," she breathed. "It's beautiful."

Saul turned to her and smiled. "I'm glad you like it."

She tore her eyes away. "It's yours?"

"No." He grinned. "It's yours."

Her heart stilled for a beat. "No way!"

"Yes, way."

"But...why?" He voice wobbled. "I don't understand." Why would you want to reward me after the heartache and grief I caused you?

"After you left me, this was my outlet, my sanity while I waited for your return."

Joy filled her from the inside out. Not because he'd spent millions of dollars and quite obviously countless hours building something for her. He really had believed she'd return. He'd never given up on her!

"Aside from Pascal and business," he continued hoarsely, "perfecting this house for your needs was my main focus."

"But I never expected—"

"You left because you craved your freedom, craved the skies." He shrugged, but there was no casual indifference in the gesture. "You couldn't do that just anywhere, not without being seen. So I bought out all the surrounding farms in the vicinity to create the privacy you would need."

He didn't say it, but the unspoken message was clear. Despite his desire that she not fly, he'd all but given her the skies, or at least a nice chunk of it. She had no reason now to leave him.

Her chest squeezed. Pressure built behind her eyes.

Saul had always been romantic. But this? It was the most amazing thing anyone had ever done for her. No. Not the most amazing. Saul had brought up her son, had taken care of him in her absence. And that was a gift she'd never be able to repay.

She sucked in a breath. "I don't know what to say."

"Don't say anything. Just enjoy."

Love for him bubbled over. "I don't deserve you. You know that, right?"

He cut the engine when they stopped beside the paving stones that led to the front double doors and turned his full attention on her. His brilliant eyes were a force field all of their own when he said hoarsely, "Do you have any idea how special you are? Do you have any idea at all how lucky I feel knowing you're here to stay?"

Before she could come up with a coherent answer he swung out of the driver's seat and moved around to open her passenger door with a flourish. "Welcome to your home."

Chapter Eleven

Wide-eyed, she clung to his arm as he led her across the front garden, halved by a path of stepping stones that were choked with white, star-shaped flowering ground cover.

Clumps of ruby and bright orange kangaroo paw softened the stark tinted-glass walls of the beautiful house. A light breeze brought with it the sweet, honeyed scent of the yellow, flowering wattle trees that grew to one side of the house, where brightly colored rainbow lorikeets shrieked and squabbled.

He keyed in a security code in a pad beside the door. She looked up at the impressive, clean lines of the building that glimmered beneath the midday sun. "How do you get anyone here to clean? And how on earth did you build at such an inaccessible site?"

He swung open the doors. "There is a helipad at the top of this building. I fly an army of cleaners in once a month." He offered her the crook of his elbow, as though he was leading her for a leisurely walk through a city park. "And the driveway was once smooth and very accessible."

"It was?"

He grinned. "To be honest, I'm not quite sure what the construction crew thought when I instructed them to chop up the road and make it almost impassable."

"So that no one would be tempted to trespass and see me. See me fly."

"Exactly." He swept out a hand. "Come, I'll give you the grand tour."

Her heels clacked on the wooden floors, the sound echoing in the vast space of sweeping glass and cream-colored walls. He'd clearly designed this with her love of open spaces in mind.

hands. She thrust it free too, leaving it to puddle on the floor alongside his discarded jacket.

Their breaths came out in gasps, sharp and more urgent as Saul pressed her against the wall beside the mirror. As her hands found and unbuckled his belt he said hoarsely, "Let me help," making short work of the button and zipper on his pants before stepping free of them.

This time it was she who spun him around. His husky chuckle was almost a groan as she pushed him against the wall. She dropped to her knees, looking up to hold his smoldering stare as she tugged down his boxer briefs and released his rigid cock.

The muscles in his thighs bunched as she leaned forward and took hold of his steel-hard shaft. As his eyelids drifted closed, she gently sucked the velvety head of his cock into her mouth, tasting it and the salty bead of his pre-cum.

He jerked. Breath whistled through his teeth. His hands dropped to tangle in her hair as he fought for control.

Her smile all on the inside, she cupped his heavy balls with one hand and held the base of his cock with the other as she suctioned his cock deeper into her mouth. Then inch by slow inch she released the hard length of his shaft.

His fingers tightened on her scalp. "Stop," he said thickly, "before I come."

She looked up. "I'm not sure I care if you do. I want to see you lose control." His eyes flashed as she finished, "I want to taste your pleasure."

Kicking his boxer briefs free, he stooped to her eye level, his jaw hard and determined. "Sweetheart, the feeling is mutual."

In one fluid motion he scooped her into his arms and straightened to his full height. In just three strides they were at the foot of his bed. He looked down at her, his nostrils flaring with need. "I want to taste you too."

She yelped as he plunked her on his bed. The next second she was giggling helplessly, passionately, as he took hold of one of her legs and

In the warmer alcove of the kitchen, she leaned against the double sink and stared out at the panorama spread before her. "I wouldn't mind stacking the dishwasher if these views were my reward."

She leaned back into his warmth as he stepped close behind her, his arms circling her waist. "I never asked you to be my maid. I'll get paid help for that."

She twisted in his arms and looked up at his serious face, his open adoration making her heart swell. "No. Don't you see? I want to do things for you, with you. I want to cook and clean. I want to be alone with you here. I want to make you happy."

His smile was all warmth and love. "What if I said having you as my lover for the rest of my life would make me the happiest person alive?"

Her chest ached, her eyes stinging with unshed tears. How had she stayed away from him for so long? All those wasted years. And already he spoke of his mortality. It was almost too hard to bear. She swallowed back heartsick anxiety and nodded solemnly. "I'd say that would make me the happiest person alive too."

He kissed the tip of her nose. "I believe the tour isn't yet over."

Moving away from the spacious living room and more intimate kitchen, Saul steered her to a curved staircase. At the bottom of the stairs, she stilled beside a life-size, female gargoyle statue that was nothing like the ugly ornaments she'd too often seen.

She reached out a hand to touch the statue's exquisite lines. "How extraordinarily beautiful."

Saul nodded, watching her closely. "That she is. But then she was sculpted by the best artist this country has ever seen. Your son."

Her touch turned reverent. Pride seared through her. Her son had created this. *Her son*! "Who'd have thought a love of Play-Doh as a five-year-old would see him become a—"

"Creative genius," Saul supplied mildly. "A master sculptor."

"Yes."

"You're looking at an image of the love of his life. Celeste Diamond."

Zahlee frowned. "*She's* a gargoyle?"

"That's debatable. Research—discreet research—suggests she's human, but has her gargoyle father's wings as a permanent legacy."

She stared at the statue, a lump in her throat. "I can see why my son loves her. She's very beautiful."

Saul nodded. "Inside and out."

She looked up at him. "Thank you," she whispered, awed and touched all at once.

His eyes softened. "What for?"

"For being there for my son, for guiding him and nurturing his creative side."

Saul released a slow breath. "I'd love to take credit, but I was never the perfect role model. He wasn't cut out for my lifestyle, though I tried for a long time to enforce it."

She covered her mouth with a hand. "Oh Saul, no."

He shook his head. "Pascal was strong, he stood up to me." He chuckled. "He made me proud and angry all at the same time. He really was my son in every way."

She turned back to the sculpture as Saul stepped behind her. She let out a sigh. "I wish I'd been there for him...for you."

"Zee. You're here now, here to stay. No regrets?"

She leaned back against the hard planes of his body, soaking up his warmth. Saul might be mortal, but she felt protected, safe with him, as she'd never felt with anyone else. Not even Steele. She twisted in his arms and looked up with a smile. "No regrets."

His stare glittered, hungry and possessive. His head dipped and his mouth covered hers in a brief, hard kiss that left her wanting more. But then he pulled away and said, "Let's get this house tour over and done with, hmm?"

She nodded, too choked up with emotion to give a coherent answer.

They went up the rounded flight of stairs and he showed her the airy guest room with its en suite, the modern home office with all the technology a person could want and the main bedroom with its huge four-poster bed and deep spa with views over the valley. Then they went through a sliding door to a balcony and she followed him up a dozen concrete steps to the helipad at the top of the building.

"Research indicates there are obstruction updrafts here generated by the surrounding mountains." He slid an arm around her and tugged her close. "Perfect for my woman. And on hot days, there are fierce thermal currents too."

Her spine tingled and itched with the need to shift and set her wings free as she stepped forward, out of his embrace and close to the railed enclosure. The green vista gleamed olive yellow under the sun's dying glare, where endless trees spread out as far as the eye could see.

She sucked in the fresh air. "You've thought of everything."

"Zee, I'd give you the world if only I could."

She closed her eyes. Her breath stilled. Her fingers curled around the rail and squeezed tightly. Oh, Saul. You wouldn't say that if you knew the truth.

And just like that, with emotional anguish tearing through her veins, pulsing with her every heartbeat, the spark of momentum to change into gargoyle became an unstoppable force that, this once, she couldn't control.

"You've done that and more," she croaked. She swung around, revealing the red haze of her vision, the physical signs she was about to shift—like it or not.

"Zee?"

Even had she wanted to she couldn't have answered his alarmed query.

Her throat arched. She snapped her eyes shut once again, focusing on the change, pushing through the pain. She wasn't a shapeshifter in the truest sense of the word, but her bones still had to soften and elongate. Her spine had to thicken and move, counterbalancing the massive wings that tore through her skin like twin daggers.

She bent over, panting, her blouse a tattered mess at her feet. But the tears rolling down her face had little to do with the terrible pain she'd endured. It was worse, much worse. "Saul, I'm so sorry," she gritted, despairing. "I couldn't stop it. I couldn't stop the change."

I should have though. I should have stopped it. Just like I should have stopped the man from forcing me to submit.

"Zee." He was beside her in an instant, his hands on her shoulders. "Please, don't be sorry. This is what I wanted for you, why I built this house. You can be a gargoyle whenever you want here without being afraid someone will see."

She managed to nod and yet still the sobs came, a panic attack that was as unstoppable as her shift into gargoyle. Her wings wrapped almost involuntarily around her naked torso, her denim jeans her only covering. "You can't love me like this." She shook her head, backing away, out of his grasp. "I'm not human. I'm not like you."

"Zee, look at me." He followed, tucking a firm hand beneath her chin and lifting her gaze to his determined one. "I love you in any form."

"No!" Denial spilled from her lips, urgent, panicked. "You just don't see, do you? You *can't* love me."

No one can.

His eyes narrowed, as though seeing her, really seeing her for the first time. She took another step back, so very afraid now, but he caught her close, keeping her still. "It's not *who* you are that worries you, is it?" He studied her, his eyes shrewd. "Zee, what happened to you?"

Chapter Twelve

Fear. Hate. Shame. Guilt. All those emotions and more that she'd carried around for so long crowded within, filling her soul with their toxins.

Blood pounded in her temples. She wanted to lash out, to hurt someone. Her hands curled into fists. "Leave me alone!"

Most of all she wanted to take away all the pain festering inside.

She sank to the concrete floor. Saul moved and sat beside her, his arms closing around her wings that enveloped her torso as tears streamed down her face and great choking sobs racked her body. Crooning sweet nothings into her ear, he stayed with her as she purged just a little of the hateful emotions held too long within.

She had no idea how long she remained folded in his protective embrace before her sobs finally subsided. She knew only that she felt lighter, as if the heavy mud clogging the underside of a favorite pair of boots had been kicked free.

She breathed in his maleness, reassured somehow by his familiar scent, which was much more pronounced while in her gargoyle form. Taking another deep, shuddering breath, she pulled back from him to look him in the eyes. "Saul, I...I was raped."

She expected helpless rage, even shocked denial. Certainly not the compassion and love that emanated from him in waves as he croaked, "A human?"

She jerked out a nod. "Yes."

A muscle in his jaw tightened. He smoothed a gentle hand over her head. "Pascal?"

"Is the result." *And the only good to come out of an impossibly terrible situation.*

"I see." His mouth white at the corners, his jaw taut with strain, he asked, "And Pascal's *biological* father?"

"He was...taken care of." She swallowed, trying not to let another round of guilt consume her. "Gargoyle law forbade he live."

He jerked out a nod. "Good."

Of course Saul would say that. He'd probably have exacted the same brand of justice, only slower and more painful.

He shifted position and cupped her face, his dark eyes searching, gentle. "You know this doesn't change anything between us, don't you?"

She bit her bottom lip. "You say that now..."

He pressed a tender kiss to her mouth. "What happened to you wasn't your fault. He—the human—was a hundred percent culpable. Not you."

"Yes." Her voice quivered. "I know that."

His eyes glittering, he took hold of one of her hands and pressed it into a fist. Guiding her hand upward, he held it over her heart. "Then believe it too."

She let out a sigh. "You're right. He might be dead, but he's already won if I don't believe in myself, in the truth."

He nodded, satisfied for the moment. Then he pulled back abruptly, stiffening as he muttered hoarsely, "Bloody hell, Zee. That's why you left me, isn't it? You thought you'd get hurt again."

A rush of dizziness assailed her. She shook her head. "No—"

"You couldn't bring yourself to trust me, a man—a human. You ran away before I could hurt you too."

"That's not true!"And yet even as she denied it, deep down she comprehended it had been a factor. Yes, she loved the freedom of the skies, but the fear, guilt and mistrust within had eaten away at her, leaving her internally scarred with doubts and low self-worth. With shame.

"Maybe you just didn't see it at the time?"

She swallowed, hurting inside. "Maybe... I just... I don't know, I—" she hiccupped loudly.

They looked at each other. The next moment they burst into laughter, the taut emotions of before instantly receding.

Saul reached out and played with a lock of her long hair. "You know, when you left me I took a good, hard look at myself. I knew unless I wanted to continue living without a conscience I had to make some serious changes to my life, had to become the man I was when I was with you."

She tilted her head to the side, hesitant. "I'm not sure I follow."

"Zee, though my reputation has been next to impossible to shake, I'm no longer the same man people loathe and fear. My business dealings have been legitimate for years now."

Her hair slid through his fingers before he captured her hand. "I've kept on with your favorite charities, done my utmost to compensate for my past." His open expression revealed quiet pride. "My donations are no longer tainted."

She could scarcely comprehend all he'd done. Her throat thickened and she wondered if he had any idea that she loved him all the more for it. "But what about your men, what about Lewie?"

He nodded. "I've kept most of them on—those who could be trusted. And though they're rough around the edges, on the whole they're relieved to be on the straight and narrow." His brow furrowed. "Lewie may be the exception."

She leaned toward him. "You know, I think you just might have made me the happiest woman alive."

He pressed a kiss onto her scalp. "And I think I just might be the happiest man alive."

She closed her eyes, sighing with bliss as his arms closed around her. His outspread fingers stroked the leathery skin of her wings. "I built this house with your love of flying in mind. But I'm betting you'd prefer to sleep under the stars too."

Her eyelids flicked open. The sun was sinking low on the far, mountainous horizon. A light breeze brushed over her skin, an autumn chill descending with the first velvet kiss of night.

She looked up at him, filled with tender love. "Must we sleep?"

Chapter Thirteen

Zahlee smiled at Saul as he parked the SUV beside the casino's entrance doors. There had never been a time she'd worshipped him more. Their renewed love for one another made her whole. Complete.

The only crack in an otherwise perfect existence was her son's absence in her life.

What she wouldn't do to be reunited with him, to tell him how much she loved him. To hold him in her arms as a mother should.

Saul moved around the vehicle and opened the passenger door. Her smile wobbled a little as she placed her hand in his and stepped out onto the warm pavement, midafternoon shadows just beginning to cast shade.

His eyes narrowed a touch, his clasp tightening as he pulled her closer still. "Is everything okay?"

Time ceased to exist. She stared up at him, her heart squeezing with emotion. "I've never been happier."

"But?" he prompted.

She shivered. Saul always had known her all too well. "I miss my son." She swept a hand out to envelop the casino. "Being here, knowing this is what helped to shape him as a person, I feel both the connection and loss even more."

He took her into his arms, his voice muffled against her scalp. "I understand. I miss him too."

The ache built within. Saul had loved Pascal like a son, she'd known that in the short time she'd been with Saul all those years ago. Her son's absence would be hurting him too, their grief was shared.

She drew back, her misty vision making her aware of the valet waiting discreetly nearby.

Saul released a heavy breath and nodded to the young, uniformed man before handing him the car keys. Then taking her hand, he led her through the revolving front doors of the casino.

"I wanted to give you the world. Obviously being reunited with your son is your world."

Her throat thickened. The pings and whirls of the slot machines were loud background noise as she rested her head against his arm with a sigh. "You were right about what you said the other day about me wanting my cake and eating it too. But it's just not likely. I'm only grateful I've got you, that I'm here with you."

His arm tightened around her just as her senses screamed alarm. She straightened, wide-eyed and alert. Saul stopped beside her, his narrowed stare scanning the vicinity.

"Steele," she whispered.

He strode toward them, tall, proud and regal. He looked amazing decked out in a fitted suit she knew he'd hate though he'd worn them in a long-ago past when he'd had no choice but to remain in his human form. He'd worked tirelessly to become a successful businessman, buying the twenty-thousand-acre mountainous land to save the dwindling gargoyle population.

Steele's nostrils flared, his eyes narrowing at the sight of her with Saul. His attention moved back to her when he came to a standstill before them. "Zahlee, we need to talk."

The room spun for a couple of seconds and she was all too thankful of the security of Saul's hold as she croaked, "Pascal...is he all right?"

Steele nodded. "Yes. He's fine."

Her pulse steadied. "Thank god," she breathed.

Steele's long, glossy black hair seemed to shimmer beneath the chandelier and dozens of downlights as he took another step toward her, his stare hardening. "Your son wants to see you."

Hope flared within, churning excitement bubbling deep in her belly. "He does?" Of course he does, why else would he have returned to the *Triskellon* clan? She chewed her bottom lip as she turned to her mute, unreadable lover. "Saul?"

"Go."

She frowned, indecisive, her emotions seesawing off the charts. Her belly cramped as a new fear took hold. "I'm not going anywhere. Not without you!" she said with a wild sob. "There must be another way. "Pascal...he...he can come here!"

Saul released her and stepped aside. "It's what you wanted. You can have your son back now. Your freedom." His stare hardened fractionally. "Your lover."

She shook her head, at a loss. "No! He's not my lover. Not anymore."

"Then he will be again," Saul stated flatly.

Hurt pressed in on her temples. Her head pounded. "Why are you doing this?"

"I was wrong to think we could be together," Saul rasped. "You don't belong with me. You never have." As though unable to help himself, he reached out, trailing the back of his hand along her cheekbone, his eyes drinking her in as though he wanted to memorize her every detail. He dropped his hand. "Goodbye, Zee."

Her heart plummeted like a stone at his resolute expression. And when he spun on his heel and strode away, something deep inside her broke down.

She deserved nothing less than him walking away from her, nothing less than the agony of heartbreak, of loss. Nothing less than what he'd experienced with her, once already.

But she knew without a doubt that his intention wasn't to hurt her. He wanted her to be free, happy and reunited with her son. He wanted her to be at peace.

She had to go after him, make him see reason. Beg him to let her stay if need be. Not having him in her life would be no life at all.

Together they'd find Pascal. Somehow she had to believe that.

She stepped after him. Steele's large hands closed over her shoulders, holding her still. "I want you back." He dismissed Saul's retreating form with a curled lip. "There's nothing here for you now."

She turned to him, her eyes burning with unshed tears. "Saul is my everything. I'm not leaving him."

Steele's eyes narrowed. "Not even for your son?" At her pained gasp he added, "Make no mistake, if you go after Saul I will leave. And I'll make sure you'll never see Pascal again."

Her eyes widened. "But you said—"

He pressed a finger against her mouth. "I know what I said. Unfortunately my honor has no place here. I'll do whatever it takes to bring you back to the clan. Do whatever I have to, to reclaim what's mine."

I was never yours!

How had she ever trusted Steele to keep his word, to honor his own decree? Tears poured down her cheeks at his betrayal, but even more fell for Saul. Right then her heart felt about to break, her soul torn right down the middle, exposing her powerlessness for all to see.

She couldn't leave the man she loved. She couldn't turn her back on her precious son.

Unrelenting numbness stole over her body, a sense of aloneness and isolation taking hold. She drew in a shuddering breath. "I'll go."

I don't have a choice.

In a daze she allowed Steele to escort her from the casino and outside to a waiting car.

How ironic. For the second time, she was leaving all her clothes, her memories, her everything behind. No. Not her memories. She'd always have them. They'd be all she'd have to sustain her.

Steele pulled her close to his side as he opened the passenger door, his arm closing around her. She didn't resist. She was void of emotion, of feeling.

"You've done the right thing," he murmured. "I knew from the moment you left I'd made the biggest mistake of my life, making you leave." She didn't answer. Couldn't. And she felt his frown as he added, "Pascal is looking forward to seeing you again."

She slid into the back seat showing no outward sign of hearing him, aware only of a searing need to see her son. A yearning that was counteracted by the devastation of leaving Saul.

Steele settled into the backseat beside her. The chauffeur accelerated and the car rolled forward, even as tears rolled down her face.

She felt Steele's gaze on her, silent and contemplative. "You really love Saul?" he asked roughly.

She sucked in a wobbly breath. She couldn't blame him for questioning her love, not when she'd abandoned the two people she loved most in the world. "I do."

I really, really do.

"A muscle in his jaw flickered as he grated, "Sometimes the greatest sacrifice is the ultimate show of love."

She swiped at her eyes, angry now. "Pretty words won't make the pain go away."

He nodded, staring ahead. Silence filled the car, a contemplative mood that lasted a good few hours. But despite her heartache, the familiar landmarks of the inland wilderness called to her soul, spoke in soothing notes like a long-lost friend.

The chauffeur looked into the rearview mirror and cleared his throat. "Sir, I think someone is tailing us."

Zahlee's pulse jumped as Steele twisted in his seat with a frown, peering through the back windshield. "It's one of Saul's men." He turned back, one of his black eyebrows raised in sardonic amusement. "We'll lose them soon enough."

Her heart sank. Of course. Once she was in the air with Steele, no car would be able to follow them.

After entering gates similar to the ones Saul had installed at his property—her property—the driver turned onto a barely discernable road, leaving the driver of the car behind them with no choice but to stay on the main road.

Zahlee leaned back, about ready to cry. It was patently obvious now. She'd never see Saul again. She'd never kiss his lips or touch his face, never be witness to the adoration shining in his eyes. Never watch him grow old.

Steele appraised her, his face brooding. His driver maneuvered the narrow lane that took them ever upward to a high summit. From there, they would leave the car and driver behind and use their wings to glide most of the way home.

Her chest ached. Home? She didn't even know where that was anymore.

After thirty or forty minutes steadily climbing, they turned onto the summit boasting three-hundred-sixty degree views. Steele nodded thanks to the driver and then they were standing alone on the ridge, turning to watch the retreating car's brake lights come on at a corner and then disappear from sight.

She turned back. A breeze played through her hair, bringing with it the scents of home—wild honey, eucalyptus, wattle and earth.

Steele placed a hand on her shoulder, his expression grave. "I know this might not feel as though you've done the right thing, but in time—"

"I'll love Saul more than ever," she burst out. She closed her eyes. Despite Steele's wrongdoing, she didn't want to hurt him too. She'd done more than enough hurting in her lifetime. But she hated him for taking all choice away from her.

She stiffened at the sound of an approaching helicopter. Steele turned simultaneously as she did at the black speck that grew ever larger on the horizon.

Steele's muscles bunched. "What the hell is this?"

Hope burst into full bloom as she stared at the shape growing in the sky, a smile spreading across her face. Saul! It was him. He'd had one of his men follow for a reason.

Minutes later a chopper landed, its blades whirring through the air. At the sight of the pilot her heart melted. "Saul," she whispered, his name whipped away by the rotors.

Steele wouldn't be going anywhere now, not without taking the risk of leading Saul into *Triskellon* territory. Oh. My. God. Had Saul set this whole thing up from the moment Steele had stated his intent?

Saul cut the engine and as the rotors slowed he opened the door and jumped out. Head ducked low, he moved fluidly toward them, to her.

His hands clasped her forearms, his gray eyes appearing even darker in his ashen face. "Zee, I wasn't ever going to let you leave me, not ever again. You know that, right?" he said above the blades' noisy rotation. "

Her jaw ached from the grin she hadn't been able to contain from the moment she'd seen the helicopter. "It just occurred to me," she conceded weakly.

He looked his age just then, looked about ready to break. "Zee, I need you."

Oh, Saul.

As the rotors finally slowed and stopped, Steele raked a hand over his face, heaving a fitful sigh. "It kills me to admit it, but you two really do belong together."

Zahlee's chest restricted. Caution restrained the joy threatening to expose itself as she turned to Steele. "We do."

Steele nodded, his expression detached. But as he tugged off his jacket and unclipped the buttons on his shirt, his hands were noticeably unsteady. "Then be happy. Go home with your lover."

Home. She knew now exactly where that was.

She glanced over to Saul. His eyes shone with love, with joy and relief. But he held back, clearly all too aware that things were unresolved.

Steele shrugged free of his shirt. His eyes locked with hers and began to redden. His face contorted with pain as his transformation into gargoyle began. He hadn't needed to change into human and back into gargoyle for a very long time. The elongation and stretching of his muscles, bones and skin would be near unbearable.

As Steele dropped to his knees, his huge, leathery wings draping from his spine, she clambered onto her knees beside him. This was not the time to ask after his well-being. She had too much at stake. Too much to lose. "Steele, you're so right. Saul and I *do* belong together. But I can't abandon my son. Not again."

Steele looked up. His chest rose and fell sharply as he sucked in air from the exertion of change. But his large hand that moved to cup beneath her chin was so very gentle when he said, "You'll see him soon enough. He came to find his mother and I won't hold him back. Not anymore."

Her vision swam. "Thank you."

His nod was almost imperceptible as he climbed to his feet. He looked down at her, his big body with his huge wings silhouetted by the darkening sky. "Zahlee, my feelings haven't changed. When you need me, you know where to find me."

Turning and spreading his massive wings, he leaped into the air, into flight.

Saul moved to stand beside her. And as Steele disappeared into the distance of the vista spread out before them, she turned to face Saul. "Have I ever told you...I love you?"

Want more (novel length) science fiction stories from Mel Teshco...
Can he protect her from his own enemy?

Nero Hart is one of only seven alien survivors, all of whom are Strazanian rares blessed with special powers. But nothing can save them from their power-hungry enemies, the Dronians, who wiped out the innocent Strazanian people. Nero and the six other rares are forced to flee their planet and survive on Earth, where they each become human and lay low. Nero becomes Jack, a nondescript male whose memories are wiped out for his own safety. But he can't escape his past forever. Recollections start flooding back, compromising his very existence. The danger further snowballs when he rescues a gorgeous human woman from her violent ex. A woman he can't seem to let go.

Brynn Monash was never a believer in fairytales, until her knight in shining armor appears and saves the day. Too bad her knight comes with scales and a fin, as well as bloodthirsty enemies determined to hunt him down. But Nero will do everything he must to keep them both alive and safe, even if he has to draw on every one of his unstable alien powers to do so.

Then Nero realizes Brynn isn't some helpless damsel in distress and there is more to her than meets the eye. Were they always meant to be together?

Chapter One of Nero

Jack winced, the deep, aching throb in his temple worse than usual. Not helped by a famous DJ who flooded Creed's Nightclub with screaming techno music. Add in the flashing neon lights above the bar, which clashed with the strobing effects on the dance floor, and Jack's headache would no doubt become unbearable.

Thankfully, his shift ended soon, but until then there was no time to do anything except mix the drinks that had patrons cramming the bar in front of him.

The tip jar was already full and Faye, one of the half-dressed bar staff, took it away with a saucy wink and replaced it with another jar.

The tips at Creeds Nightclub never ceased to amaze Jack. That they were meant for the staff but most often went into Creed's deep pockets was yet another irritation that didn't sit well with Jack.

Up until recently he'd been content with his minimal wage. What did a thirty-something single man without a social life need when he had a sagging roof over his head and paper-thin walls to keep his insignificant supply of worldly crap together? That he scraped enough together to pay the rent and expenses was as much from his solitary existence than it was from any foresight.

He assumed he'd always been a take-one-day-at-a-time kind of guy. But with his barman days turning into weeks and the weeks into months, his future was beginning to look set in stone and a pay rise the incentive he needed to continue one mundane day into the next.

Not that he doubted for a second the owner of the establishment, Creed—or Greed, as the staff called him behind his back—would be agreeable to giving him a wage increase. The too-handsome, smooth-talking, dark-haired wanker was all about profits and his own needs.

But then Jack had a knack at being persuasive, and after the monotony of making drinks he almost looked forward to testing his influence with Creed.

Jack handed two Whiskey Sours to a blonde whose fake tits almost spilled out of her white top, her long, even faker lashes fluttering. She leaned close, eyeing his bare chest as she slurred, "Your drinks are ahhmazing!"

It wasn't the first time he'd heard that line and it wouldn't be the last. He smiled and nodded, aware of her "take me home" vibes. Some nights he felt like a rock star, and took advantage of the plentiful supply of ladies on offer. What single, woman-loving man in his right mind wouldn't?

Most of those ladies had even been fine with his shabby house in the downtrodden suburb of Skeeds, along with his one-eared, black tomcat that had wandered in one night and never left. But then he had the awkward morning after confrontations to deal with and it was a toss-up sometimes if the pleasure of a short term fuck was worth the next day irritant of a meaningless separation.

You're such a class act. He winced. He had no idea when or why he'd become so cavalier about women...about life in general. In the grand scheme of things he was lucky to get laid. He was an average looking man heading toward middle-age, admittedly with a full head of sandy-blond hair and a damn good body. Luckily for him on the latter since the barman uniform consisted of nothing more than black pants and a tie, and sturdy shoes of course.

That he plied people with drinks for a living meant he didn't need to worry about imposter syndrome. He was nobody, a nothing, a man whose skills consisted of pouring beers, tossing bottles into the air and shaking up frothy drinks.

Meanwhile Creed was becoming one of the richest men in the city, his flashy cars and a mansion on the river Dahrt, attesting to it. Creed didn't mind flaunting it, either. He loved collecting priceless artifacts from all over the world. He loved even more to show them off on a high display case above the bar like a mantelpiece, which no one could reach.

Tonight there was a pair of ancient, crisscrossed swords showcased in velvet, and what was probably a Ming vase. All of which sat untouchable behind thick plate glass. That Jack was inexplicably drawn to the weapons was another mystery he'd rather not solve.

Had he been a psycho in the past? An axe murderer?

He had no idea who he was or where he'd come from. He only remembered waking up on the street in the dark, then stumbling into Creed's well-lit bar where self-preservation had made him ask for a job. That he'd got one still mystified him. He'd looked like shit and hadn't even had the foresight to invent a better name than Jack.

His shift finally ended and he wiped the alcohol off his hands on a clean cloth behind the bar.

"See you tomorrow night," Suzie shouted above the music. She was another one of the eleven other bar staff kept busy on a Friday night.

"I'll be here," he mouthed back. He had no place else he needed to be.

Other than finally speaking to Creed.

After pulling off his worn leather jacket from a staff coat rack hook, he headed toward the spiral staircase in the corner of the club, which would take him to Creed's office above. The partial level was a recent addition after Jack had started work here a little over six months earlier and the place had taken off.

Creed's favorite entertainment was overseeing the milling patrons on the ground floor below, his floor to ceiling glass windows giving him a perfect vantage point. He spent more time in his office than he did at his fancy mansion on the river. No doubt the man got a hard-on imagining the endless exchange of drinks for cash.

Jack pulled on his jacket with a wry smirk. Creed might make all the money and have the looks, but it rubbed the man the wrong way that he didn't get anywhere near the same attention from women that Jack did. Not that he understood the logic behind it. Creed had everything, Jack had...nothing.

He ignored the bouncer standing to one side of the steel door, the man's thick arms crossed and his feet wide apart, his face expressionless and his boredom all too apparent. Jack arched a brow. Perhaps serving drinks wasn't half-bad after all.

He rapped on the door, and Creed swung it open with one hand, his other clasping a bottle of half-empty, premium vodka. He grinned manically as he stepped aside and said, "Jack, come in!"

Creed slammed the door shut after Jack, the immediate silence inside the office nothing short of a fluffy cloud after the violent din of the nightclub. The quality of soundproofing was superb.

Creed lifted a dark brow. "I guess your shift is over." He swigged some of his vodka, then asked, "What can I do for you, Jack?" Creed swaggered over to his huge desk, then flopped onto his leather chair and chugged some more from his bottle. He looked at him. "Well?"

"I want to discuss my future here."

Creed sat up straight, his eyebrows drawn together and his gaze suddenly alert. "You're not thinking of leaving?"

A familiar, tingling warmth filled up behind Jack's eyes. He had no doubt it was caused by his headache. They seemed worse when he was around other people, particularly obnoxious ones. Noise just exacerbated the condition. Working at a crowded nightclub with inebriated patrons wasn't his most sensible career choice. "That would depend on a pay rise."

Creed gaped, then slowly blinked at him. "Is that what this is all about?" He snorted out a tinny laugh, the sound oddly mechanical. "I've been meaning to discuss that with you anyway, but you coming here saved me the trouble. Name your price."

Jack's skin prickled suddenly and felt too tight, and he resisted closing his eyes and massaging the serious tingling going on behind them. Instead he held Creed's stare and said, "I want fifty percent more than what I'm getting now."

"Son of a bitch! And here I thought you didn't give a crap about money and worldly possessions." Creed's laugh pitched higher, as though hysteria threatened. "The women certainly don't seem to care." He slapped the table. "Done!"

Shock for a moment held Jack in its grip before he finally managed to crack a smile. He only wished triumph reigned supreme. He'd gotten what he'd wanted. Except...money wasn't really what he wanted. He wasn't into material wealth.

So what exactly do you want?

If only he knew. He'd been getting more restless lately, his abstract memory flashes becoming more frequent and disturbing, right along with his headaches. He sighed. It only highlighted his need to be alone. Well, most of the time. He was still a man. He still enjoyed short-term physical intimacy.

Creed leaned back in his chair, his arms loose by his sides and the vodka bottle dangling precariously from his hand. When his eyes took on a vacant look, Jack slipped back out the door before Creed thought better of his offer. If Jack had second thoughts then it stood to reason Creed would too. But surely not even Creed would go back on his word, not without looking like a total ass.

Jack was lost in thought and descending the spiral steps when all hell broke loose. Someone shouted warning, and glass shattered, then cascaded onto the floor in a jingling mess. Jack paused and looked up at the priceless display shelf, where a young man with afro hair and a glinting jewel in his nose was hanging off the shelf like a monkey, one of the swords in his hand.

Impossible. The glass was all but unbreakable, and the weapon was surely too heavy for the monkey-man with his slight build. The ancient sword had probably once been wielded by huge, muscled gladiators of old.

The music ground to a stop and bouncers came running.

Monkey-man flashed a grin and dropped gracefully to the ground, his bare feet seemingly impervious to the sharp glass. "Stop where you are," he said calmly, his voice clear. "This sword is now mine."

Everyone froze, and the thief snorted out a laugh before he broke into a run, heading toward the nearest exit.

Jack looked at the motionless crowd. Not even the bouncers had moved.

What the fuck?

His eyes met the bold gaze of a brunette woman who was standing near the edge of the dancefloor. Her mesmerizing green stare glowed and for a moment he was transfixed by a surge of familiarity. Then his temple throbbed twice as hard, the back of his eyes stinging until he was forced to drop his gaze.

Pain immediately diminished.

Creed slammed open his office door to survey the carnage below. When he took in the shattered glass that revealed his missing sword, his face flushed a deep red and his whole body drew tight. "Don't just stand there!" he roared. "Get whoever took my sword!"

The bouncers managed to look at one another, their stares still dazed and a little vacant. But otherwise they didn't seem to have the ability to move.

Jack gritted out an obscenity and raced down the last of the stairs, taking off after the afro-haired piece of shit. Pushing past the crowd, he ran out the front doors and onto the rain-wet sidewalk, where streetlights barely infiltrated the darkness. He paused. He mightn't love Creed but a thief was even lower on his personal ladder of dislikes.

That Jack coveted the swords for himself only heightened his anger.

Movement caught the corner his eye. "Stop!" he shouted.

The thief ran faster.

Jack's gaze narrowed. He'd grown accustomed to people listening to him, it had become as natural as breathing. But why he thought a thief would do the same was every bit as silly as the sky turning green.

A sudden shockwave of pain hit his brain front and center, and it took everything he had to ignore it and break into a sprint. Damn it, he really did deserve a pay rise after this!

He leaped over a wooden pallet and onto the asphalt road. At this time of night there were very few cars. It was only after he bounded over a deep pothole without breaking stride that shock set in a little. Where had his speed and stamina come from? He had no idea when he'd last run. He couldn't recall much of anything before finding work at Creed's.

That he'd been numb in mind and spirit had stopped him from caring or questioning it...until now.

He'd yet to break a sweat, his heartrate and breathing slow and steady as he turned left and then right down alleyways, quickly gaining on the sword thief. His fitness really didn't make any sense. His only exercise these last six months had been screwing the many available women from the club.

The thief stumbled and slowed, and Jack gained enough ground to launch himself at him. *Oomph.* The air knocked out of Jack's lungs as he hit the afro man who staggered and fell forward, the sword slipping free as he scrambled back.

The thief's eyes squinted. "What the fuck is wrong with you, Nero? Are you *trying* to blow our cover?"

Jack straightened. "Cover? *What* cover?" he growled. "And who the fuck is Nero?"

The other man's eyes glowed, an odd amber-orange that surely couldn't be natural. "Shit. I should have known. You haven't been awoken yet." He shook his head and mumbled, "Guess that is why Sienna tracked you down."

"Jasper, that's enough!"

Jack spun around to lock eyes on the same brunette he'd seen earlier. She wore a black bodysuit that fit her svelte body like a second skin, the silver buckles on her knee-high boots gleaming under the streetlights.

He blinked at her as recognition once again pulled at his senses. He shook his head, his temple throbbing. "How did you get here so quickly?"

She shrugged. "I ran. Same as you."

The pain in his head intensified, as though his skull was shrinking against his brain. He ground the heel of his hand against his brow. "Can someone please explain what the fuck is going on?"

The woman—Sienna—approached him. "Are those headaches of yours getting worse?"

He grimaced. "What would you know about that?"

"I know everything about you, Nero Hart."

A white-hot bolt of agony shafted through his head and he fell to his knees as unconsciousness beckoned around the gray fringes of his vision. "My name is Jack!"

"Jack who?"

"I don't remember. I don't recall anything before working for Creed."

"And why do think that is? And did you ever wonder why that man accepted you as a barman, giving you cash-in-hand work with no credentials and no identification?" She stopped a few yards away, folding her arms across her chest. "I'll tell you why, Nero. You can influence others, it's the universal trait shared by all us rares, along with our ability to shift shape. You just happen to be the best."

Pain splintered through his skull and he groaned as jarring memories threatened to surface and overwhelm him. It made sense now why Creed had so easily given into his demands for a pay rise.

"You're pushing him too hard," Jasper muttered.

Even through the wall of pain a thought surfaced. What was the thief still doing here? Shouldn't he have scampered off with the sword?

Sienna sighed before she looked at Jasper and said, "Nero's own influence has stopped his recall. It's also likely to have saved his life being that he'll be the first of us the Dronians will hunt down and try to kill."

"Dronians?" Jack asked. His breath hissed as an image of a stone-gray reptilian creature filled his head. Though it walked upright on its powerful hind legs, it was about half the size of a human…and twice as strong. Those same hind legs had the ability to launch the Dronian twenty feet into the air, while both upper and lower limbs sported razor sharp talons that could eviscerate its victim within seconds. "What the hell is going on?"

Sienna's boots crunched on some loose gravel as she took another couple of steps forward, and Jack sensed her crouch beside him even before he forced his bleary eyes on her.

She smiled, her face serene while her green eyes glinted with sympathy. "As you probably heard, I'm Sienna. Our little thief over there is Jasper. We're two of the seven who escaped Strazan and our enemies to hide here on Earth. You make three, Nero."

"I don't believe you," he croaked.

Her smile turned into a grimace. "You can't escape your memories forever, Nero. We need you fully awoken now."

"What? Why?"

"Because without you, none of us will survive."

For your exclusive FREE story: Her Dark Guardian, and where you can find out when my next book is available, as well as other news, cover reveals and more, sign up for my newsletter: https://madmimi.com/signups/121695/join

Check out my website – http://www.melteshco.com/

You can also friend me on Facebook at https://www.facebook.com/mel.teshco

Or my author Facebook page at https://www.facebook.com/MelTeshcoAuthor

And occasionally on Twitter at https://twitter.com/melteshco

Contact me: melteshco@yahoo.com.au

If you enjoy my books I'd be delighted if you would consider leaving a review. This will help other readers find my books ◈

About the Author

Mel Teshco loves to write scorching hot sci-fi and contemporary stories with an occasional paranormal thrown into the mix. Not easy with seven cats, two dogs and a fat black thoroughbred vying for attention, especially when Mel's also busily stuffing around on Facebook. With only one daughter now living at home to feed two minute noodles, she still shakes her head at how she managed to write with three daughters and three stepchildren living under the same roof. Not to mention Mr. Semi-Patient (the one and same husband hoping for early retirement...he's been waiting a few years now.) Clearly anything is possible, even in the real world.

Want more Mel Teshco books?
Science Fiction:
The Virgin Hunt Games:
The Virgin Hunt Games volume 1
The Virgin Hunt Games volume 2
The Virgin Hunt Games volume 3
The Virgin Hunt Games volume 4
The Virgin Hunt Games volume 5
The Virgin Hunt Games volume 6
Dragons of Riddich:
Kadin (prequel - book 1)
Asher (book 2)
Baron (book 3)
Dahlia (book 4)
Wyatt (book 5)
Valor (book 6)
The Queen (book 7)
Alien Fugitives:
Nero (book 1)
Jasper (book 2)
Sienna (book 3)
Damaris (book 4)
Zander (book 5)
Jaire (book 6)
Epello (book 7)
Alien Hunger:
Galactic Burn (book 1)
Galactic Inferno (book 2)
Galactic Flame (book 3)
Coming soon
Galactic Blaze (book 4)
Nightmix:

Lusting the Enemy (book 1)
Abducting the Princess (book 2)
Seducing the Huntress (book 3)
Winged & Dangerous:
Stone Cold Lover (book 1)
Ice Cold Lover (book 2)
Red Hot Lover (book 3)
Winged & Dangerous Box Set (all 3 books in the series)
Dirty Sexy Space continuity with authors Shona Husk and Denise Rossetti:
Yours to Uncover (book 1)
Mine to Serve (book 6)
Ours to Share (book 8)
Awakenings series with Kylie Sheaffe
No Ordinary Gift (book 1)
Believe (book 2)
Homecoming (book 3)
Standalone longer length titles: (50k-100k)
Dimensional
Mutant Unveiled
Shadow Hunter
Existence
Standalone novellas and short stories: (15k-40K)
Identity Shift
Moon Thrall
Blood Chance
Carnal Moon
Contemporary:
Desert Kings Alliance:
The Sheikh's Runaway Bride (book 1)
The Sheikh's Captive Lover (book 2)
The Sheikh's Forbidden Wife (book 3)

The Sheikh's Secret Mistress (book 4)

The Sheikh's Defiant Princess (book 5)

The Sheikh's Fake Fiancée (book 6)

The Sheikh's Royal Widow (book 7)

The VIP Desire Agency

Lady in Red (book 1)

High Class (book 2)

Exclusive (book 3)

Liberated (book 4)

Uninhibited (book 5)

The VIP Desire Agency Boxed Set (all 5 books in the series)

Box sets with authors Christina Phillips & Cathleen Ross

Sheikhs & Billionaires

Taken by the Sheikh

Taken by the Billionaire

Taken by the Desert Sheikh

Resisting the Firefighter

Standalone longer length titles: (50k-100k)

Highest Bid

As I Am

Standalone novellas and short stories: (15k-40K)

Stripped

Clarissa

Camilla

Selena's Bodyguard (also part of the Christmas Assortment Box)\

Anthologies:

Down and Dusty: The Complete Collection

The Christmas Assortment Box

Secret Confessions: Sydney Housewives

Don't miss out!

Visit the website below and you can sign up to receive emails whenever Mel Teshco publishes a new book. There's no charge and no obligation.

https://books2read.com/r/B-A-ZFLB-AKGI

BOOKS 2 READ

Connecting independent readers to independent writers.